*"Item number sev...
walnut Victorian cradle, folks,"*

the auctioneer cried out. "What do I hear for it?"

"Oooh, it's a steal," Marcella said, raising her paddle in the air.

Brent's eyes rounded in horror. What was she planning to do with a cradle? "Cella—"

"Shhh!" she whispered as she continued a bidding war with a fellow in front of them.

"Marcella, you're not planning to fill that thing, are you?" Brent asked bluntly.

Her face clearly showing distress, she turned toward him. Her arm dropped, and she placed the paddle on her lap.

"Sold to the gentleman in the yellow shirt," the auctioneer intoned.

"Cella?" Brent grabbed her arm.

She rounded on him. "Yes, I have plans for a cradle."

Dear Reader,

*Spellbinders!* That's what we're striving for. The editors at Silhouette are determined to capture your imagination and win your heart with every single book we publish. Each month, six Special Editions are chosen with *you* in mind.

Our authors are our inspiration. Writers such as Nora Roberts, Tracy Sinclair, Kathleen Eagle, Carole Halston and Linda Howard—to name but a few—are masters at creating endearing characters and heartrending love stories. Their characters are everyday people—just like you and me—whose lives have been touched by love, whose dream and desire suddenly comes true!

So find a cozy, quiet place to read, and create your own special moment with a Silhouette Special Edition.

Sincerely,

Rosalind Noonan
Senior Editor
SILHOUETTE BOOKS

# MARTHA HIX
# Every Moment Counts

*Silhouette Special Edition*

Published by Silhouette Books New York

**America's Publisher of Contemporary Romance**

To Carl
for his faith, inspiration and expertise

SILHOUETTE BOOKS
300 East 42nd St., New York, N.Y. 10017

ISBN: 0-373-09344-6

First Silhouette Books printing November 1986

America's Publisher of Contemporary Romance

Printed in the U.S.A.

## MARTHA HIX

is the mother of two grown daughters and lives in San Antonio, Texas, with her husband and a menagerie of pets. When she's not busy writing, she enjoys outdoor activities and researching geneology. What doesn't she like? Dieting and housework.

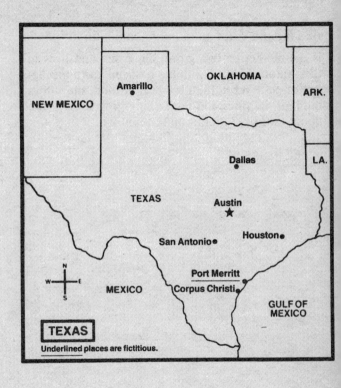

OKLAHOMA

NEW MEXICO

ARK.

Amarillo

Dallas

LA.

TEXAS

Austin

San Antonio

Houston

N
W  E
S

Port Merritt

MEXICO

Corpus Christi

GULF OF
MEXICO

**TEXAS**
Underlined places are fictitious.

## Chapter One

*Great, a party in full swing before dusk!* Marcella Parker lugged a bag of groceries from the car seat. After pushing the aged sedan door closed with a hip, she trudged her weary bones past the flashy automobiles blocking her side of the driveway and on toward the duplex into which she had moved the prior day. The people next door had been quiet to that point. Not so now. Loud music flowed from the residence adjoining hers. It looked as if her hopes for neighbors who observed the golden rule were dashed.

Well, she simply wouldn't let that bother her. *Don't expect everything to be perfect,* she scolded herself while walking alongside a white convertible. She had been extremely lucky to find these spacious, but affordable, seaside accommodations in a community the size of Port Merritt, Texas.

Without warning uneasiness struck as a deep-chorded woof, followed by loud barking, blasted the spring air. Oh, no! She hastily set the heavy bundle of goods on the steps leading up to the U-shaped deck. Her cat was outside, easy prey for a stray dog!

Marcella's eyes widened as she rounded the corner. A Doberman pinscher, lips curled back to expose huge, snapping fangs, leaped toward the window ledge. Toward her Siamese! Tail and hackles raised, Mona Lisa hissed in defense.

Run! was Marcella's first instinct. Almost instantly the impulse was replaced by rationality. Be calm, she ordered herself. Dogs know when you're scared. Maybe the Doberman was too intent on his quarry to notice her, and at least Mona Lisa had the edge of vertical distance—the high windowsill. Marcella shrank away, her hand grasping backward for the railing that was nowhere within reach.

But the Doberman, turning, spotted her. Pink from his gums showed; a line of saliva flew from his mouth. He charged, lightning fast, his long legs and mammoth body bounding across the planks.

Bracing herself for the attack, she had only a last-ditch chance. "Stay!"

He screeched to a stop. Stubby tail wagging, the dog sat back on its haunches, very near her. Limpid brown eyes looked up at Marcella.

She breathed a sigh of relief and mustered her faculties. "Good doggy."

All of a sudden a long tongue snaked out of the tan-framed mouth and flicked Marcella's calf. Not quite over the trauma, she tentatively extended her arm to let the animal sniff the back of her hand. She was rewarded once more with a wet lick, this time on her palm.

"Ugh." Kneeling down, she patted the sleek black fur on the Doberman's head. "Who are you? Where'd you come from? Where's your master?" To an answering whine, Marcella kept up the one-sided chatter. "Doesn't she—"

Something about this dog said the owner was male. Had to be. This was not a lapdog, by any stretch of the imagination. And she couldn't help wondering about the owner. She envisioned someone ruggedly male. Whoever he was, he had given the dog loving care, had trained it to be gentle with humans. But...evidently he was irresponsible. Otherwise he wouldn't let the animal roam freely.

"Doesn't your master know a big baby like you could get in trouble being let loose? Given the chance, that cat of mine would scratch your eyes out. Or worse, I could have been the dogcatcher."

The Doberman inched forward on its stomach, dropping its jaw on Marcella's foot.

"You've been naughty. You scared Mona Lisa and me, too," Marcella confessed, taking a liking to the canine who was now as docile as a lamb. "If I didn't love dogs, I'd be awfully upset with you."

As if he understood, he climbed to his feet, ducked his head and moved several yards to disappear through a dog door, which she had never noticed before, cut into the wall of the adjoining duplex. At least the whereabouts of his master was cleared up.

Should she speak with the owner about the dog's well-being? No, best not. Marcella decided against playing the buttinsky with her new neighbors.

Marcella rolled her eyes and walked over to the ledge. The Siamese objected with a nervous hiss as Marcella took the cat into her arms. Then, careful not to let go of her wiggling charge, she retrieved her groceries and struggled into the safety of her house.

"Looks like you're going to be housebound, sweetie, unless I'm outside with you." Marcella put her sack on a table and loosened her grip on the cat.

With her usual ungrateful air Mona Lisa growled in her peculiar Siamese way and jumped to the floor, traipsing haughtily to a hiding place behind the sofa.

Marcella tried to shut her ears to the loud noises coming from the common wall's opposite side. She wasn't going to let anything keep her from being happy.

Picking the sack up again, she looked with satisfaction around the antique-filled living room. Even though she had moved in only one day before, there was a place for everything and everything was in its place. Calm, order and quiet were important to her.

At once a bloodcurdling scream tore the air as the BOOM! of something evidently large and in flight slammed against the dividing partition. Pictures and shelves rumbled. A crash and a splintering of glass echoed in Marcella's ears.

She turned and her hand flew to her mouth, groceries spilling. A vase had fallen from its place of honor on a shelf and was scattered in jagged pieces on the floor. Tears filled her eyes. The vessel wasn't an heirloom; it had been won long ago by her father at a carnival. But it had meant the world to her.

Brushing away teardrops with the back of her hand, she crossed the room and knocked on the wall to alert the party goers that they were out of line. In answer she received muffled laughter.

Anger filled her. This was the last straw! She was going to talk with those people. She charged the thirty steps separating front doors.

Her three impatient rings of the doorbell were answered by a tall flaxen-haired man of about thirty. His broad chest, tanned a rich shade of bronze and pelted with crisp brown hair, contrasted with the white, drawstring pajama bottoms that rode low on his narrow hips. Leaning into an easy stance, he cocked his palm against the doorjamb while a grin played across the planes of his mustached face.

For a split second Marcella's purpose for being there slipped her mind, and she responded with feminine instinct. My, he was handsome. Then, with inwardly directed irritation, she reminded herself not to put any stock in exterior varnishing.

"Well, hello," he said in a smooth Texas drawl.

"I'm your new neighbor, Marcella Parker," she stated crisply.

"Brent Coulter's the name. Welcome to the neighborhood."

"Didn't you hear me knocking on your wall?" She stretched to alleviate the disparity in their heights. His, she guessed to be at least a foot taller than her five-three. "What is going on over here?"

"Karate match. And no, I didn't hear you. I was reading in my bedroom."

"Reading?" she repeated incredulously, looking past her tall neighbor to the two average-looking, kimonoed men who stood behind him and were watching her boldly.

"Yeah, he's too good for us," the wiry-framed one commented. "We're beginners."

Marcella dug in her heels. "Mr. Coulter, if I could speak with you in private...."

The other man started to say something, but the Adonis interrupted. "Please come in. Then you'll have my—" he lifted a thick brow "—undivided attention."

"Wooo," the karate enthusiasts chorused.

She shot withering looks at the two boors.

Brent inclined his head toward the door. "Okay, guys. Vamoose!"

"Come on, Allen. Let's go," one replied as he grabbed a key ring from a nearby table that held a stack of mail.

"Shoot, the party's just getting good," Allen grumbled under his breath, smiling at Marcella as he also departed.

Brent slammed the door behind the two men. "Welcome to my humble bachelor quarters." He grinned, apparently pleased with himself for imparting his marital status without having to be asked.

The flirt! And Marcella wasn't the least impressed with his bachelorhood as she moved into the living room, pointedly sidestepping a hideous bearskin rug, head and snarled fangs attached.

*His* walls were all intact, of course, she noted with disgust. None of the walleyed hunting and fishing trophies had fallen down during the karate match.

Beyond her pique over the vase and the noise, killing defenseless animals for sport was not her idea of entertainment.

Brent's eyes, as cool and green as the Caribbean Sea, were appraising her, missing none of her one-hundred-pound frame. "Are you married, Marcella?"

"No, I'm not." She shouldn't have answered so quickly, she realized. She didn't want to give the impression that she was interested in him. The only thing she wanted was to have her say and get out of his house. At least that's what she told herself. But it was next to impossible to ignore his half-clothed body. Though miffed at him over the party, she was, after all, a breathing female.

Her flaxen-haired neighbor's gaze slid from the tip of her toes past her well-worn safari shorts and oxford-cloth blouse to the top of her black hair as he gestured toward a leather sofa. "Have a seat."

She lifted her chin. "No, thank you. What I have to say won't take long, Mr. Coulter."

"Brent," he corrected, crossing the room to turn off the stereo system.

The sudden quiet had a calming effect on Marcella, and she breathed easier. If he wanted to be called "Brent," she wouldn't quibble over that. She nodded toward the wall separating their two houses.

"Brent, we're going to have to set up some guidelines we can both live with."

"Sounds thought provoking." A wry tone shaded his voice. He grinned, the action crinkling slight lines that radiated from the corners of his eyes. "What sort of guidelines? For coffee klatches? Borrowing sugar?"

"No, not guidelines for those sorts of trivial pursuits." Crossing her arms over her chest, her attention riveted to a Chinese vase sitting safely on an end table. She seethed at the reminder. "Guidelines about loud noises. And destroyed property."

Brent's brows knitted. "Destroyed property?"

"Yes. Someone hit the wall a few minutes ago. A vase fell off my wall shelf and broke."

"I guess the karate match got a little out of hand." He appeared genuinely apologetic. "Look, I'll be happy to buy you another one."

Her eyes flickered, and she swallowed back the lump in her throat as she thought of the shattered keepsake. "It can't be replaced."

"I'm sorry it got broken. But it's not like someone died or something." When she bristled he appeared regretful. "That came out wrong."

A door opened in the background, then closed again. The Doberman she had encountered earlier pranced into the room toward Marcella. Remembering her former meeting with the overgrown baby, she regarded the man who was in her estimation handsome and irresponsible and insensitive.

"Another thing—you shouldn't leave your dog outside unattended. As friendly as he is toward people, someone might steal him."

"It's never been a problem before. Fred stays in the yard."

"I have a cat, and he treed her. Before I found out how gentle he is, he frightened both of us."

"Again, my apologies."

A cold nose touched the back of her thigh. Marcella turned, leaning down to pat the dog's head. She wasn't going to take her anger out on Fred.

"Is, uh, your cat a Siamese?" Brent asked in a strange voice from behind her.

She faced the man once more. "Yes, she is. Why?"

"While she was left outside *unattended*, she prowled through my trash can."

Marcella flushed, realizing that she had been as irresponsible as he. "My turn to be sorry," she mumbled, her voice tinctured with embarrassment as the dog nuzzled her ankle.

"Get lost, Fred," Brent ordered emphatically.

"*He*'s not bothering me."

"She." Brent smiled, then bent over to rub the Doberman's back, a shaft of lamplight accentuating the play of shoulder and arm brawn. "Don't you know how to spot a male animal?"

Marcella did a slow burn at the sexual connotation of his tone. "I most certainly do. And I also know how to spot when a conversation is going nowhere." She turned from him and made for the door. "Good night!"

Quickly he darted in front of her, stopping her forward motion. "Let's clean up the loose ends of the conversation before you leave. I'll make restitution for the vase, keep a lid on the noise and harness Fred." Irritation written on his face, he ducked his head down toward hers. "And in return you might try working on your diplomacy act a little more. That is, if you're intent on keeping peace with me. Remember, we do have to live next door to each other."

"I'll keep my distance if you will."

"Agreed." He stepped back. "Now maybe we'll both have a good night."

Marcella fled from his house. Once in the solitude of her home, she bolted and chained the front door. As she leaned against the wooden barrier for support, her raging anger slowly turned into a smoldering fire.

She was furious with Brent and his friends for having broken her vase. She was furious to learn that her next-door neighbor was a Casanova, ready to turn on the charm for any available female.

But then, she reminded herself, he hadn't said anything that out of line. Had she conjured up emotional danger signs? Maybe! Maybe her heated reaction had been uncalled for. And just maybe he had been right— her attitude needed work. Of one thing she was sure: she didn't trust Brent Coulter.

Her devastating relationship with Jim Turley had broken her heart into a million pieces. When it had healed Marcella had promised herself that no man would ever hurt her like that again. Common sense and practicality erected a barrier around her heart and emotions, keeping good-looking, irresponsible men at arm's length.

Her move to the south Texas coastal town of Port Merritt, population ten thousand, was intended to be a new start, a chance to be in unexplored surroundings and to throw aside old memories of Jim. From him she'd gained a keen insight into the dearth of character beneath the surface of a handsome face.

In the aftermath of her and Jim's relationship, Marcella's small circle of friends in Houston, thinking that she needed to forget one man in the arms of another, had arranged dates for her. Oh, some of the men had been nice. Two or three of them had been better than nice. But she hadn't been able to trust her heart. And none of them had lighted a spark in her soul.

From the ashes of her loveless existence, she had devoted even more of her energies to the one thing that mattered. Her banking career. And tomorrow she started a new job as vice president and petroleum expert at Goodman National Bank. At least the encounter with Brent Coulter had kept her mind occupied with something besides the looming first-day-at-work jitters.

Walking to the utility room, Marcella collected broom and dustpan, then went to the living room. She sorted her thoughts while sweeping up shards of glass. No, money couldn't replace the vase, but it was only a possession. Nothing could shatter all the cherished memories she had of her deceased father. Nothing.

The staples purchased earlier were neatly put away in the pantry. Marcella checked doors and windows, then tucked Mona Lisa into the folds of her arms as she switched lights off. Holding the self-ruling cat to her chest, she made for the bedroom. No matter how early, she needed the peace of sleep.

"Stay out of the man's trash, or we'll both be in trouble." Once settled in the mahogany four-poster, she Eskimo-kissed a cold nose. "We have a good life, don't we?"

"Mmmeehh."

"Crabby old spinster."

To avert a skin scratching, she grabbed a taloned paw. A feeling of emptiness went through Marcella as she thought of the life she led.

"We're both crabby old spinsters, aren't we?" she asked, expecting no reply. "But we're doing fine. We don't need any tomcats in our lives, do we, sweetie?"

All things considered, she was blessed. She would gather her cozy little world around her and be thankful for her many advantages. She had a nice home, even if it was rented. This seaside duplex on the outskirts of town had been leased for a mere pittance, considering the spacious square footage. Its unusual design, modern on the outside but blending easily to her own style of homey decorating on the inside, was a godsend. And she was willing to work diligently at the profession that had sustained her through heartache and disillusionment. That's all she needed for happiness.

If only she could convince herself of that fact.

Thinking of Marcella, Brent Coulter stood in his kitchen and swirled a glass of club soda and lime. He intended to keep his good-neighbor promises. He was a man of honor.

He couldn't blame her for being upset. The guys had been making a helluva commotion, and Fred had been running loose. Those things hadn't been important before; the adjoining bungalow had been vacant since he'd moved in four months ago.

He regretted that crack about spotting a male animal. The remark was made innocently enough, but it came out all wrong. When Marcella had bent over to stroke ol' Fred, she'd given him a blood-warming view of her derriere as it tautened the material of her godawful shorts. Damn! Her mama should have warned her not to do that in front of a man.

His head rolled back as he recalled the flowery yet light scent of her perfume. His mind's eye drew a picture of her. She was beautiful. He loved long jet-black hair. She was tiny, could probably fit under his arm just right. And she was rounded in places where a woman ought to be rounded. While beauty meant the least to him, Marcella appealed to him—but not only physically. High-spirited women had always fascinated Brent.

In his thirty years of living he had never been a quitter. And he wasn't going to start with Marcella Parker. Brent never backed down from a challenge.

Unexpectedly a man loped into the kitchen. "Where's ever'body?"

"Hmm?" Brent was remembering black-fringed eyes, as blue as the Texas sky.

"Get the stars outta your eyes, boy!"

"I thought I told you to leave," Brent said irritably.

"Huh?" His employee was obviously perplexed.

"Party's over."

"Coulter, I was planning to leave, but you darned well didn't tell me to go!" Jerry Hagen hitched up his trousers. "What's the matter with the hotshot president and chief executive officer of RSK Petroleum Corporation? I've never known you to break up a karate match."

Brent gathered his thoughts. "Guess you were on the telephone when Marcella came by."

"Marcella? Who dat?"

"My new neighbor."

"Oh. I thought I heard a woman's voice when I let Fred out of the study." Jerry wiggled his red brows. "Looker or...?"

"That's none of your damned business."

Jerry pulled a beer from the refrigerator, then tossed the pop-top in the vicinity of the brimming garbage can. His voice was abruptly serious. "Say, Lefty, I need to talk with you before I leave."

"Don't call me Lefty. I hate it."

"Debbie calls you Lefty."

"Only by virtue of being my sister."

"All right, already." The geologist perched on the counter. "I've been on the phone with the tool pusher, in case you didn't know. Amigo Drilling's getting antsy. What are we going to do about the Rollins Field?"

A proud smile lit Brent's face. The Rollins Field. His baby. From the first day he had set foot on an oil rig as an eighteeen-year-old, he'd been determined to be an independent oil man. A wildcatter. Petroleum was in his blood. Nothing was sweeter in his nostrils than the acrid stench of crude oil ... it was the incense of power.

Despite the reverence he attached to the subject, Brent's response was facetious. "Oh, I don't know. Drill for oil?"

"You know, it isn't necessary to put up a front with me. We're in this together, even if I am the employee and you're the owner." Jerry shook his mop of red hair. "Have you read today's drilling report?"

"Of course." Brent downed his drink. "Hard shale and traces of hydrocarbons at forty-eight hundred feet."

"Blast it, Coulter, ten thousand acres of the best black gold in Texas is lying under that ground. Five or six hundred feet more is all we need, and the exploratory well *will* come in. We can't give up now."

"Let me explain finances. It'll cost as much to drill another six hundred feet through that shale as it did to reach the five thousand we budgeted for." And if cash flow problems aren't solved soon, drilling will have to stop, Brent purposely didn't add. If he used his readily available personal funds, the exploratory could reach fifty-one hundred. Max. Then where would the company that he'd created be? He would be wearing a barrel—and crude oil still would not be gushing.

The reed-thin geologist must have sensed the problem. "Have you checked with the bank in Corpus Christi that loaned you money for start-up?"

"Hagen, I've done everything but get on my hands and knees to them. They don't put much stock in our drilling logs. With all the bankruptcies that've been happening in the oil industry, they're leery of extending another large chunk of money to an independent."

"You could go to Sneed Goodman," Jerry suggested hesitantly, very hesitantly.

"Never!"

"Just because he's Vicky's father doesn't mean he won't loan you some greenbacks."

The less said about his former wife, the better, Brent seethed. He started to pass Jerry, making for the living room. But Jerry, not to be ignored, stopped him.

"Coulter, don't forget—Goodman likes you, and you do have several accounts at Goodman National."

"I'll pulse the banks in Houston."

"You're not going to let her ruin your life, are you?"

Brent's answer was truthful and swift. "My ex-wife has nothing to do with it. You know I'm not carrying a torch for Vicky. And hell will freeze over before I'll grovel at Sneed's feet. He warned me that I was getting into the petroleum industry at a bad time. I respect that man as much as I do my own father, and I won't—hear me, will not!—let him tell me 'I told you so.' Understand?"

"Aye, aye, Cap'n."

Brent turned from the geologist and grabbed a package of cigarettes from atop the refrigerator. Why had he mentioned his father? Thinking about Albert Coulter brought to mind one thing: failure. As far as petroleum exploration was concerned, the elder Coulter had an amazing ability to sniff out fossil fuel. Brent blew a stream of smoke toward the ceiling. When it came to making the right decisions financially, his father had been behind the door when they passed out smarts. He was determined not to follow in his father's footsteps.

"Pride goes before the fall, Coulter, and you're making a mistake if you let your ego stand in the way of bringing in the Rollins Field." His friend caught his arm as Brent threw the match into an ashtray. "Keep this in mind: if the Corpus bank won't consider upping your loan, I don't think Houston will be any more receptive."

"Let me handle the worrying, and you take care of interpreting the logs." Brent's hand sliced the air in a gesture of finality. "And I thought you were leaving."

"I'm going, I'm going."

The silence of his home surrounded him as Brent dropped onto an oversize easy chair, slamming his eyelids closed. He loathed being reminded of Vicky.

Their marriage had been a nightmare. He had had the mistaken impression that marriage was supposed to be something like his parents shared. The man wins the bread and cherishes the woman. The woman lights the home fires...and keeps the bed warm. Okay, it was an old-fashioned notion. And he wasn't harboring any illusions about Today's Woman. His former wife, Victoria Goodman-Coulter, M.B.A., was a prime example of that woman.

Maybe he had been selfish and expected too much. Back then he'd tried to compromise. Never once had he demanded that Vicky soil her hands with housework or have dinner on the table. He was happy to pay a housekeeper to do those chores. What he had wanted was a little attention, a tad of a sense of humor on his wife's part...and the closeness he craved with an intensity that knew no limits.

He couldn't stop the whip of resentment that tensed his muscles at the mere thought of being trapped in another miserable relationship.

Although he was soured on wedded bliss, he wasn't soured on women. He liked them—no, *adored* them!—as long as mutual compatibility bloomed. And they understood up front that he wasn't going to be led around, again, by a nose ring. His epitaph was going to read: "Brent Coulter, Bachelor."

And if things progressed past the neighborly stage with Marcella Parker, that was what he intended to make clear. Real clear. He nodded as though the action would solidify his reasoning.

His line of sight fell on the table opposite him. Suddenly he felt a niggling of guilt. He had made a heartless remark about Marcella's broken vase. He had caught the shadowing of her eyes when she said it couldn't be replaced. Tomorrow he would buy her the finest crystal vase that he could find. No, that wasn't such a good idea. Why not give her something that had sentimental value to him? He considered rushing next door. But that wasn't a brilliant idea, either. Undoubtedly Marcella wouldn't appreciate his presence.

Brent furrowed his brows. Doggone it, he wished that he hadn't asked Jerry to leave. Better yet, he wished Marcella Parker hadn't left. Alone and lonely he wouldn't be able to get his mind off his temporary financial woes.

He was scared. Damned scared.

Fred clunked over to his side, nudging his hand before dropping her jaw onto her crossed paws. Brent scratched man's best friend's ear, and he felt better.

Why was he being maudlin? he asked himself. Something would turn up. RSK wasn't dead in the water, yet. He'd known what he was getting into when he started. After all, financial risk to find petroleum is the name of the wildcatter's game.

And he still had an ace in the hole.

So why not kick back and think about something even riskier? Shoving a pile of magazines from the ottoman, Brent propped his feet up, planted his elbow on the armrest and braced his chin on his knuckles.

What was his next move with Marcella?

## Chapter Two

The next morning Marcella donned her best dress-for-success suit, then swept her hair up in a tight bun at the crown of her head. She glanced at the acorn-finial banjo clock on the bedroom wall. Heavens, it was only six-thirty! She wasn't expected at Goodman National Bank until eight. Talk about first day eagerness, she thought wryly. What could she do to keep occupied? Unpack that last box of out-of-season clothes? No, she might run her panty hose. Read the newspaper? She hadn't started home delivery. Where was she going to get a paper?

"I'll go out and buy one," she mumbled to herself.

She opened the hallway door leading to the garage. Mona Lisa was pilfering through Brent Coulter's garbage can!

"What are you doing out here?" She grabbed the cat and started picking trash up from the concrete floor. "I didn't let you out."

"Talking to me?"

Marcella whirled to the sound of a deep, resonant voice. Brent dropped something that appeared to be small clippers into a metal box, then dusted his hands as he started toward her. He was certain to chastise her for being an irresponsible animal owner, she figured.

"I'm afraid Mona Lisa's been caught in the act again."

Brent smiled. "She's forgiven."

"I'll make sure it doesn't happen again," Marcella said, while scooting the cat into her house. To his credit, he hadn't reminded her of that promise made last night. Still determined to have as little to do with the aesthetically appealing Mr. Coulter as possible, she avoided eye contact with him. Her finger pressed the garage-door opener and she started toward her car, which was still out on the street. "Please excuse me."

He loped after her, catching her arm. "Marcella, we got off on the wrong foot last night. I don't want to be at odds with you. What do you say to starting over?"

"We didn't get off our feet at all last night," she answered coolly.

Brent's eyes narrowed. "Wouldn't it be easier for both of us if we were on speaking terms?" When she didn't immediately reply, he said, "Duplexes are extremely close. Too close for comfort when their occupants are at loggerheads. Wouldn't you agree?"

"Yes." She nodded. "You're right."

"If you're not in a hurry, would you stay and have a cup of coffee with me?" He grinned cordially. "I've got a fresh pot."

"Well..." Considering his offer, Marcella looked at her wristwatch. "I need to get to work." She gave him a small smile. "First day."

Brent's lips widened to display perfect white teeth; his eyes twinkled. "Just one cup of coffee while I apologize." He held the appropriate number of fingers to his forehead. "Scout's honor. I won't make you late."

"All right." Marcella chuckled. "One cup."

Stepping back, he showed her into his hallway and down to the messy kitchen. In no time at all he had served two cups of delicious coffee and was sitting across the round table from her. A cloak of silence fell over the breakfast area.

Marcella couldn't help but wonder about Brent Coulter. She knew absolutely nothing about the man except that she didn't like him—no!—she didn't trust him. He frightened her. Yet she felt compelled to look at him, really look at him. As she studied the rather tender expression on his handsome face, her tension eased a fraction.

She toyed with her coffee cup and forced rational thoughts. Her mind warned not to rely upon her heart. He was her neighbor, that's all. A very handsome neighbor. Remembering past disillusionments, she vowed not to be influenced by his outer appeal or by the ease of the moment. But resolve or no resolve, she was powerless not to notice the thick shock of flaxen hair that crowned his chiseled cheeks, firm jaw and deeply clefted chin. He wore jeans and a soft, faded cotton shirt. And on him, they looked marvelous.

"I'm sorry about last night," he said.

"I acted pretty wretched myself," Marcella heard herself say. And vow or no vow, she couldn't help wondering if that rye-colored mustache was as soft as it appeared.

"By the way, I have a peace offering for you." He swiftly rose and went into the living room, returning in no time with the porcelain vase that she'd seen the night before. Her eyes widened. It was filled with a kaleidoscope of beautiful wildflowers! "With my heartfelt apologies," he continued, handing it to her.

"I—I can't take your vase," she said, aghast.

"I insist."

"It's much too valuable," she protested.

"So was yours." Sincerity rang from his voice. "Marcella, don't deny me a chance to make amends to you. Accept it and the spirit it's given in."

Unaccustomed to having anyone do nice things for her, she was overcome by his thoughtfulness. This sterling facet to his character bridged the gap dividing her and Brent. She smiled, and her gaze collided with his sea-green eyes as he handed her the vase.

"I'm touched by your offer, Brent." Her voice was warm as she lifted the orange, blue and yellow blossoms from their holder. "I'll take the flowers and the spirit they're given in. Thank you."

"You're welcome." Brushing a left index finger across the tip of an aristocratically straight and fine nose, he winked an eye. He reached for a tall glass tumbler that sat on the counter. "Let's put them in this. You don't want to get your pretty blue suit wet."

Conversation trailed into companionable silence, and each one enjoyed the spirit of giving and receiving . . . and of neighborly camaraderie.

"Tell me about yourself, Cella," he prompted finally. "I haven't seen you around Port Merritt before."

No one had ever shortened her name, much less given it a decidedly Latin inflection. She liked it. A lot. *If you're not careful, you're going to have more than neighborly interest in this man!*

"I just moved here from Houston. This is my first day at Goodman National Bank." She needed, for her own sanity, to remove herself from Brent's mesmerizing presence. "Since Port Merritt is such a small town, I'm sure you're acquainted with the bank."

"Yeah." A strange look crossed his face, and he rose to pour more coffee. "Good luck on your first day."

"No more caffeine for me." She picked up the gift and started for the door. "I have to go now. I don't want to be late. And thanks for the flowers—" her sight landed on the Dallas Cowboys tumbler "—and for the 'vase.'"

He caught her arm and a tingling sensation swept through her.

"I forgot something, Cella."

She turned, her sight filling with the light-colored material of his shirt and with the dusting of chest hair that peeked above the top button. Her eyes swept upward to his marvelous eyes.

"I never told you that I'm pleased to meet you," he continued, his voice a caress.

"Thank you, Brent."

* * *

On the way to Goodman National Bank and during the brief training sessions given by each department head, Marcella tried futilely to forget about Brent Coulter. Though he had shown there was more to him than a shallow surface, and though she had been wrong to equate Brent with Jim, she couldn't allow herself the folly of trust.

At long last sitting at her desk, she scanned her expensively furnished private office. Her vision centered on the dominant feature of the room: a life-size portrait of Our President, as the brass plate read. His knee resting on the top edge of a desk, Sneed L. Goodman's arms were crossed over that leg, one hand holding a pair of black spectacles as he leaned forward. The pose was deceptively relaxed. Piercing brown eyes stared back at his newest vice president as if to say "I'm watching you, young woman. We here at Goodman National pride ourselves on our personal service to our depositors. Mind your p's and q's."

I will! she promised with first-day eagerness.

Marcella always performed her duties with minimum direction. She patted the pile of work in the brass in-basket. Awaiting her was the chore that all bankers hate: collections. She picked up a computer printout of overdrawn corporate checking accounts. Scrutinizing the list of companies assigned to her, she blew a heavy stream of air through her pursed lips.

Since most customers kept a minimum of funds in a non-interest-bearing account, Goodman National's policy was for the officer in charge to extend the courtesy of a telephone call to those in an overdraft status. As gently but as firmly as possible, she cajoled twelve depositors into making a stop by the bank to "cover this oversight."

She tapped her gold pen against her teeth, reading the thirteenth name. "*RSK Petroleum Corporation. Starting account balance: $5,212. Overdraft amount: $25,003. High balance Year-to-date: $11,954. Number of overdrafts Year-to-date: twenty-five."

"Not bad for April, RSK Petroleum Corporation," she commented dryly. She wondered briefly about the asterisk. *Must be an entry typo.* None of the other accounts were so noted, and she couldn't recall any special instructions for such a mark. After punching seven telephone digits in quick succession, she waited through eight rings.

"Hello," a female answered, then she yawned.

What a way to answer a business telephone, Marcella surmised. That was harsh. Port Merritt wasn't Houston. She had a lot to learn about dealing with small-town mores.

"This is Marcella Parker of Goodman National Bank. May I speak with the financial officer, please."

"I guess that's me. Hi, I'm Debbie."

Rolling her eyes, Marcella began her spiel. "...and will you be able to make a deposit today?"

"Gee, I dunno."

Marcella heard scrapes through the line that sounded like an emery board sanding across a fingernail. "Debbie, may I please speak with your supervisor?"

"He's tied up right now." The youthful voice giggled. "Every time I say that I can just picture Lefty tied to a chair with a rope!"

Try as she might, Marcella couldn't help chuckling. She, too, had conjured up the same sort of visions at times. Not of Lefty, naturally.

"Um, Debbie, RSK has a deficit totaling almost twenty thousand dollars. Is there an account we can transfer money from? Or can you give me wire-transfer instructions?"

"Golly, I dunno. Can you call back after a while?"

As if she was speaking with a child, Marcella asked, "Is there anyone else in the office I might speak with?"

"Nope."

"Please ask 'Lefty' to call me. If there's a problem with finances, perhaps a short-term loan can be arranged. But if I don't hear from him by eleven sharp, I'll be forced to return the checks. And I'll have to charge the account a handling fee for each one." She placed her pen on the desktop. "Can I count on you to give him my message?"

"Oh, yes, ma'am."

Marcella had serious doubts as to the girl's reliability, but there was no alternative. Needing advice, at eleven o'clock she stopped by Mr. Goodman's office. He, as well as Wayne Alvarez, the executive vice-president, was out until late in the afternoon. She was third man on the totem pole. The decision was hers. Chewing a thumbnail, she tried to telephone RSK again. No answer.

It would be irresponsible to let such a large amount of money out of the bank. Hard experience had taught her to be suspicious of oil operators; too many banks had folded in the recent past when bankers didn't keep on top of matters. She didn't relish doing it, but in neat, precise script she penned "Return all checks. Charge account. M. Parker, V.P."

She dropped the printout by bookkeeping. The department head, a woman on the down side of fifty named Bernice Prothro, gave the list a quick once-over before dismissing Marcella with a flick of her hand.

The afternoon flew by as Marcella was introduced to fellow employees and bank customers. She felt exuberant. Everyone at the bank, with the exception of cranky Bernice, was relaxed and friendly. The atmosphere of laid-back esprit de corps was a pleasant, unexpected job perk.

By five o'clock she had dusted off the bottom of her in-basket. Again she smiled at Mr. Goodman's portrait. He was awesome, but she respected him and his achievements. He'd had the foresight to make the correct moves with Goodman National by catering to the petroleum industry of south Texas. While oil-and-gas banking wasn't as lucrative as in boom times, the bank was solvent and growing. Total assets far outstripped what would be expected in a small community. It showed in bank size and lavishness. And to a certain extent in salaries.

Her experience in the oil-and-gas department of a large bank in Houston had landed her this vice presidency. And she was grateful for the step up from that assistant-vice-president position.

As an eighteen-year-old, she had started as a new-accounts representative. Endless nights of studying for her degree, the hard-won respect of her peers and her dedication to banking only made her more proud of her accomplishments. She was surviving...and succeeding.

Picking up the material that the personnel manager had left, she began completing the necessary employment forms. The one lying on the bottom was for her personnel file. The first part was the usual. Name, address and so on. After filling in twenty-nine for her age, she hesitated. The bottom part wasn't that easy.

Married: "no."

Person to contact in case of an emergency: "none."

That about summed up her life. And it started a chain of recollections. She had no family, hadn't since her father had died when she was ten years old. The courts had placed her in an orphanage. Too old to be considered of prime adoptability, she had whiled away the years yearning for the return to a semblance of family life and dreaming of a future home, husband and children to call her own.

At least she had a house filled with antique furniture and cooking smells. That goal had been accomplished through hard work and lots of counting nickels and dimes. And not counting on men like Jim Turley.

But she still wanted a husband, someone nice who would share the same interests and hobbies. He wouldn't have to be handsome. He wouldn't have to be rich. He would have to love her. And from that love...those babies she pined for. Marcella was trying her best to ignore the fact that time might not always be on her side.

Oh, don't sit around moping, she told herself. Think positive. It was time to leave for the day, and the comforts of home sounded like heaven!

Suddenly the door flew open. Her secretary, Sharon Bates, ducked her head through the entry. "Ms. Parker, the president wants to see you in his office."

When Marcella entered the sumptuous office of Sneed L. Goodman, she saw his scowling countenance.

"Ms. *Park*-er!" he spat out. His face was livid with rage. "What is the meaning of this?" He held aloft the overdraft computer run, shaking the paper in the air. "What explanation do you have for authorizing the return of RSK Petroleum's checks!"

Explanation? Marcella seethed silently, irritated that her superior would lash out at her in anger. It wasn't standard practice to be called on the carpet over such a routine matter. Although she was quaking inside, she marshalled her dignity.

"Mr. Goodman, as vice president of this bank, I made a decision based on past experience."

He threw the run to his desk. "The reputation of a valued customer of this institution has been maligned."

*And my authority undermined.* "I accept full responsibility." Her voice was calm, despite the blood pounding in her temple. "I'll contact the clearing house immediately and settle the matter."

"It's too late for that. They've already returned the instruments to the payees." He eyed her critically. "Why didn't you ask for instructions in handling overdrawn accounts?"

"I *was* given instructions, sir." Bernice Prothro had gone over the procedures with her. Although she had endeavored to be meticulously careful during the training session, Marcella realized that she could have forgotten something. Probably while she was musing over Brent Coulter!

"Then what does this mean?" He tapped a finger against a line of type. "Look at RSK Petroleum Corporation."

An asterisk was flush left against the company name. Earlier she had chalked it up to an entry error, a typo. None of the other depositors had such a mark by their name. Now she realized that she had been remiss in her duties by making such an assumption.

"I have no idea, Mr. Goodman."

"This means that funds are to be transferred from other accounts when a deficit situation occurs." Goodman whipped off his glasses. "As an experienced banker, you should have inquired if you didn't know."

"I stand on my record." She paused only fractionally before she said, "And, Mr. Goodman, this is only my first day with Goodman National."

"You're right." He exhaled loudly, and his voice lowered to normal. "To the best of my knowledge, you have a fine background. I'll overlook your lack of judgment, but I don't know how the president of RSK is going to react."

The part about judgment was hard to swallow. Her professional abilities had never been questioned in the past. But the blame was hers, and she had no intention of making matters worse by petty defense tactics. The best way to handle the situation was to be extra careful of her duties in the future.

"Thank you," she replied.

"It will be necessary, however, for you to contact RSK Petroleum Corporation and make full apology for your actions."

"That goes without saying ... sir."

"Good night, then."

If she had anything to be thankful for, it was that the bank was closed and she could make straight for the sanctity of home. Yet, once she got home, the haven of her surroundings did little to lessen the reproof's pain.

The four walls seemed to close in on her. Thinking fresh air might help ease her humiliation, she hurried into her swimsuit and grabbed a towel before proceeding to the duplex's private beach area.

Marcella loved the ocean's pungent odor, the briny taste of the sea and the caw of sea gulls above the lapping water. They gave her a sense of peace with man and with nature. With any luck those sights, sounds and smells would work their healing powers that evening.

Settling onto the sand near the tide line, she hugged her knees. Her face tipped to the unseasonably warm April sun that shone in muted tangerine hues against the western coastline. She leaned back, planting her palms in the sand. Eyelids closed, she took several deep, calming breaths and forced pleasant thoughts to replaced troubled ones.

The flaxen-haired man from next door floated into her mind. Would it hurt to daydream, for only a moment, about Brent? That morning, it had been so easy, so very easy, to communicate with him. The surf's roar pounded rhythmically against the white beach, as if to call "Cella...Cella." Gradually her tension ebbed with the tide.

"Evening, Cella."

Brent. Brent! Her eyes flew open, her sight filling with his muscle-packed hairy legs. The fading sunlight at his back, he stood, tree tall, with bare feet widespread. One hand at his hipbone, the left clutched a large paper bag. Shading her eyes, she looked quickly past the swatch of black cloth that strained across his lean hips. Heavy whorls of downy hair circled his concave navel, fanning upward to his granite-hard chest. She gazed higher. His shoulders appeared even wider than the previous evening, his biceps even more powerful.

"Mind if I join you?" he asked, setting the paper bag onto the sand. His gorgeous green eyes held the blue of hers.

But as before her practical mind warned her impractical heart not to wade into the undertow that was pulling her into danger. She jumped to her feet. "I'm afraid I wouldn't be good company tonight."

"You look as if you could use a friendly ear." His hand caught hers. "And I could, too. I had a terrible day."

As though a mirror were reflecting her need for companionship, Marcella discovered a matching vulnerability in his eyes. She sank back onto the sand, clutching her toes. "I guess I could stay for a few minutes."

Brent dropped to his knees beside her. "You first," he said.

Marcella blinked her eyes in surprise.

"Talk about it," he explained.

To open up and discuss her problems with anyone, and especially with a man, was foreign to her. But Brent seemed different than Jim, who had never been interested in anything but his own creature comforts.

And with Brent she felt an unexplainable trust that superseded the veneer coating her inner thoughts.

"Promise you won't breathe a word? It's about my job."

He nodded affirmation. "Tell me about it."

"I'm in trouble at work. I turned back some checks on—" She paused momentarily. "Before my error was discovered the clearing house had already processed the returns."

Elbows braced against a knee, Brent brushed his chin. "I'm sure it'll be okay," he tried to soothe.

"I don't know. Mr. Goodman is awfully upset with me. And I still have to answer to the customer," she admitted. "I have no one to blame but myself. But it hurts way down deep. There's never been a blemish on my career before."

"Sounds to me like the customer is just as much at fault."

"I won't go so far as to say that." Remembering the telephone conversation with Debbie, Marcella rolled her eyes. "I called them about the overdraft. You would not believe the birdbrain they have working in their office. Apparently she didn't give her boss my message before or after she left the office unattended. Anyone who would hire such a girl is a terrible businessman." Hearing her own words, Marcella flushed and dropped her lashes. "I shouldn't have said those things."

"Maybe not. But it's a natural reaction to a tense situation."

"Believe me, I'm not as loony as I sound. My only excuse is the moon's full, and I'm a holy terror when the moon's full."

"Forewarned." He caught her hand and squeezed reassuringly. "Let's not let it spoil our supper."

"Supper?"

A bucket of chicken and a bottle of wine materialized from the brown bag. "Bought in your honor."

Laughter bubbled from her throat, and the tension of the moment was broken. She'd let tomorrow take care of itself! Tonight she would toss caution to the sea breezes.

"You are not only a very kind man, you are simply amazing! But just what would you have done if I hadn't been home?" she asked with a teasing note in her voice.

He tore a piece of golden-brown chicken breast and held it to her lips, his fingers grazing the smoothness of her cheek. His voice was soft. "Sweetheart, don't ever question destiny."

Her skin burned where he touched her. Somehow she managed to swallow. Were they destined for each other? Of course not. But wouldn't it be nice to make-believe... She watched Brent uncork the Pinot chardonnay and declined when he offered her the wine bottle.

He tilted back his head. Fascinated, she watched his strong throat work as he tipped the golden liquid to his lips. She felt drawn to him, to his kind and tender heart. He had shown that there was more to him than she had thought originally. And she couldn't deny the butterflies fluttering in her tummy. But deep down she knew he wasn't her type. Oh, Lord, give me strength to fight my feelings, she prayed.

They ate in silence for a few minutes, mutely watching the sun sink below the horizon.

"So, tell me about yourself," Brent finally said into the hush of the newly dark night.

"I, um, I don't want to discuss me."

"Then what do you want to talk about?"

You! she yearned to answer, flicking sand from her leg self-consciously. She wanted to hear what made him happy and what made him not so happy. Did he like to haunt junk stores and antique auctions? Did he like home-cooked meals and the family life? What about cozy nights in front of a flickering fireplace? Was he a spur-of-the-moment seducer or a lover ruled by the regimen of convention? Did he believe in love?

"I'm waiting," he reminded.

Practicality, however, wouldn't allow her to tell him what was on her mind. "Um, I don't know."

A lazy smile pulled at the corner of his mouth as he lowered himself to his side, never taking his eyes from her. She clutched her toes, breaking the visual contact that both captivated and unnerved her.

"Cella," he urged in his melodious pronunciation, "take a look at that moon." His nail grazed the line of her jaw. "It's a lover's moon."

"I've never heard that," she murmured, grabbing the wine and taking a swallow.

"Shh. Don't break the spell." He whispered her name softly. "I want to kiss you."

Something wild and wonderful was going on inside her as their gazes welded once more in the deepening shadows of darkness. She was floating on the gentle waves of enchantment when slowly, oh, so gradually, he leaned closer to wipe a trace of moisture from her lips, his tender touch arcing a charge of current between them. There was nothing, no one in the entire world, but the two of them as her feminine instincts took over.

Fluidly he guided her to the sand, the weight of his body fitting her beneath him. He was wonderfully warm, and she inhaled deeply his distinctively male scent interlaced with the faintest hint of woodsy after-shave. She felt a delicious tremor wind through her to settle in the center of her femininity and to remind her of the sweet basic element of life that is the difference between acceptance . . . and fulfillment.

The crook of his left forefinger lifted her chin. "I could get used to the feel of you in my arms," he crooned, above the crash of a breaker.

*Oh, I could, too!*

A deep groan vibrated from his throat as he framed her face between his big hands, his lips parting slightly as his mouth descended. Breathlessly aware of the arousing sensations that threatened to overcome her, Marcella struggled against the black magic of her passion.

They were moving much too fast, and she couldn't let this happen. Swiftly her fingers flattened against those lips . . . that mustache. Oh, my, it was silky.

"Please—" her voice faltered "—no."

"Why?"

"W-we don't even know each other."

His teeth gently nipped her palm, his thumbs exploring the shell of her ear, the hollow of her throat. "What better way to get to know someone, Cella?"

"I—I can't handle a casual affair," she whispered, crying out for sanity amidst her rubbled defenses.

"It's good for the disposition. Especially under—" his gaze lifted upward "—the full moon."

Her palms wedged at his chest. "Let me up."

"Is that really what you want?"

"Yes."

Loudly forcing the air from his lungs, he craned away and rolled over in the sand. With his head resting on crossed arms, he closed his eyes. "You want to talk, Marcella. So talk."

Still reeling from his touch, she didn't know what to do next. Small talk seemed ridiculous. But it had been her idea that they find out more about each other.

"What do you want out of life, Brent?"

"A cold shower."

"You've never told me what you do for a living, Brent," she persisted.

"I run a nonprofit organization."

"A charity?"

"I was being facetious. It's not supposed to be a nonprofit organization. It's a corporation."

By his clipped replies, she sensed he didn't want to discuss his business affairs. "You said you had a bad day."

"I had to have some excuse to get you to talk with me." Brent was watching her fingernails as they raked through the sand, then his gaze met her. "A man could drown in the blue depths of your eyes, Cella."

And she could have drowned in the green depths of his, but that was dangerous water. "Have you ever been married?" she asked, not about to wade into that tide.

"Yeah. Divorced, too." The tense silence stretched before he asked, "You?"

"I've never been married." Her eyes sparkled. "Confirmed bachelorette?"

"Oh, heavens no," she answered quickly. "When the right man comes along, I won't let him get away."

Brent's face paled. "Apple pie and wedding rings aren't what they're cut out to be, Marcella. Believe me, I know."

"You sound bitter."

"Yeah, I'm bitter." Jackknifing to his feet, he towered above her. A tiny muscle flickered at the corner of his mouth. "Marcella, I like you, like you a lot. I'd like to spend some time with you, be your friend—and more. But if we become more than neighbors, let's get one thing straight: don't get your hopes up on me."

"Why, you pompous—" She couldn't think of an appropriate name that was ladylike to utter. "Brent Coulter, don't get your hopes up on *me*."

Brent gathered bucket and bottle. "Let's call it a night."

A chill breeze whipped Marcella's face as he jogged away. And she let him go, sensing that he needed to be alone. As she did. The breakup of his marriage had hurt him terribly. His stark words had pointed that out. Possibly he wasn't over his wife. Quite possibly.

Yet her heart ached for him. She realized that pain and suffering stained his soul as indelibly as it did hers.

Marcella considered her own state of mind. What were her own feelings? She was fascinated with Brent, even though he was sold on himself. Considering all the factors involved, fascination was best stifled.

There was no denying the physical attraction sparking between her and Brent. But where would she be after the spark of attraction fizzled?

The answer was simple. In another dismal situation reminiscent of three years ago. She had trusted Jim completely. In the beginning he had been smooth and charming. He'd told her that he loved her and had misled her into thinking they would marry. He had insisted on a "trial marriage," and being gullible, she'd moved in with him. But when push had come to shove he hadn't wanted to make a lifelong commitment. The day he'd snarled that he had absolutely no intention of making their relationship legal, she'd been cut to the quick.

The backwash had been hell on earth. And a lesson well learned. She had thought. Before she'd met Brent her emotions had been as tightly guarded as the gold in Fort Knox. Before Brent.

Nonetheless she was going to be strong, and she was not going to fall prey to Brent Coulter's charm. She had no use for the "more" that he'd mentioned.

In his study, Brent swept his arm across his report-littered desk, sending papers flying in every direction. He was furious with everything, but mostly with himself, for letting his bitterness overrule his head. Damn! He'd been making headway with Cella. Running his nails along his scalp, he straddled a chair. He needed to take it slow and easy with her. She was skittish as a colt, and he'd been . . . pompous.

The fact of the matter was that he was letting the disillusionment of his marriage play with his head. Cripes, he had done everything in his power to please Vicky. Back then he had touched and wooed, kissed and hugged. And paced the floor trying to understand her. And himself. But she hadn't been interested in him. She was gung ho for her career. Nothing else.

That didn't stop him from wishing that he had made her happy. Bruised ego aside, he respected Vicky. She was a decent person and deserved more out of life than what she was settling for.

And Marcella deserved better than what he had dished out, he admitted.

While he'd wanted to set the ground rules, he knew he had gone about it the wrong way. Surely he could handle himself better than that. He felt ultrasensitive to what she was thinking and feeling. Why? He barely knew her; she barely knew him. He rubbed his jaw, searching for an answer.

He was lonely. He hadn't been getting as much out of his personal life as he would have wished. There were plenty of women around for good times but he wanted more. He needed the magic of companionship, friendship and trust. And with time and patience he felt that sort of a relationship would grow between him and Marcella.

He was going to march himself over to Cella's house and ask if they could, once again, start over. As soon as he answered that damn telephone.

Fifteen minutes later Brent had showered and was searching for both his hard hat and the Bronco keys. There was trouble at the wellhead. Big trouble. The visit with Marcella would have to be shelved for the time being. Damn!

Marcella was determined to whip her feelings back into the proper perspective. She had a professional mistake to rectify and a life to lead. Sans Brent Coulter. By burying herself in her responsibilities she would forget him.

To her surprise and relief, Sneed Goodman walked into her office the next morning, patted her on the back and, smiling cordially, said, "Sorry I flew off the handle yesterday afternoon, Marcella. I realize you had GNB's best interest at heart." Wonders never cease.

But that didn't stop the anvil that was pounding in Marcella's head. She picked up the telephone to make that dreaded explanation and apology call to RSK Petroleum.

"Delivery for Marcella Parker," a fresh-faced young man announced from behind two-dozen scarlet roses. Marcella slowly lowered the receiver and, somewhat hesitant, accepted the flowers.

Along with the delicate buds came a note. Marcella committed the inscription to memory.

"I'm sorry. Forgive me? Let's be friends. Brent."

She clutched the card to her chest. By accepting his offer she would be taking a perilous chance with the fragile threads of her equanimity. Should she disregard her past heartbreak and give Brent the benefit of the doubt? What about his feelings for his former wife?

Her mind envisioned him once more, envisioned his face as he had consoled her the night before. She needed his presence in her life, the helping hand he had offered. But would he be willing to settle for friendship? It wouldn't hurt to be his ally, as long as she kept reminding herself that amity was the basis for and the extent of their relationship.

And who's to know what might blossom between two friends, a voice in the back of her skull reminded. Aren't respect and trust the best basis for...?

"I'm a glutton for punishment," she muttered. "Get back to work."

To her chagrin she was unable to reach RSK Petroleum by telephone and extend her apologies.

After the lobby closed for the day, Marcella's secretary, Sharon, stopped by her office and asked in a friendly voice, "Ready to call it a day, Ms. Parker?"

"Am I ever. And you?"

"Oh, yes!" Sharon chewed her lower lip as if contemplating her next words. Then a smile lit her dimpled face. "You don't know how much I appreciate the opportunity to work for you, Ms. Parker."

"You work with me, Sharon, not for me." Wagging a forefinger, she returned the girl's grin. "And I asked you to call me Marcella, remember?"

The secretary waited for a minute, brushing her honey-blond page boy behind first one ear, then the other. "Ms. Parker, I mean, Marcella, I hope you don't think I'm out of line, but, well, I heard what happened with Mr. Goodman and his former son-in-law."

Marcella moaned inwardly, dying a thousand deaths. "No wonder Mr. Goodman was upset. He didn't tell me RSK was a family enterprise."

"It's not really. Vicky's ex-husband owns RSK. Sneed Goodman has nothing to do with the company. And as for the president, don't worry about him. He scared the heck out of me when I first came to work here. It didn't take me long to find out what a nice person he can be." Sharon turned around and loudly said, "Good night, Bernice!"

Heels clicked away from the open doorway.

Marcella's brows knitted. "What was the meaning of that?"

"Bernice Prothro was eavesdropping." Sharon looked indignant, loyalty to her new supervisor evident. "She should've called your attention to RSK when you turned in the printout to her. She knows funds are supposed to be transferred from one of their other accounts when RSK's overdrawn."

"Mrs. Prothro isn't responsible for my mistake." Or was she? Marcella wasn't in the habit of forgetting important details such as transfer authorization codes. She decided to keep an eye on the head bookkeeper. "I accept full responsibility."

Sharon's voice was abruptly low and soft. "Marcella, you don't have to be an island unto yourself. I'm here to help you. It isn't necessary to do it all alone."

"I appreciate that." Sharon had a way about her that inspired Marcella's confidence. She was glad the secretary was in her corner. "I should've asked for your help yesterday." In the past Marcella had always been self-sufficient and too aggressive when it came to the challenges of her career. "I suppose I'm accustomed to doing everything on my own."

"No more of that. Agreed?" They shook on the pact, then Sharon started fiddling with the hem of her suit jacket. "Were you able to contact Brent Coulter?"

Marcella's brows knitted again. In a town the size of Port Merritt it was reasonable to assume that everyone knew everyone. But what a strange question. "Why would I contact Brent Coulter?"

The secretary's brown eyes rounded. "Why, he's the owner of RSK Petroleum."

If it were humanly possible for blood to rush out of the body and to pool around the feet, Marcella couldn't have felt any more sapped of strength. Brent. Oh, dear heavens, those things she said last night. By now he was sure to know what she had done to his company!

How was she ever going to face him again?

## Chapter Three

Brent Coulter shifted from one foot to the other as he waited for Marcella in the bank parking lot. Mad as hell, he was deciding whether he should murder her or merely cripple her. During the long hours at the drilling site the night before, all he had had on his mind was getting back to be with her. Before stopping by his office this afternoon and finding the note to return Marcella's call, Brent thought he owed her an apology about the previous evening, and had even put on a suit and tie with the idea of impressing her. He had yearned to ease the loneliness of his heart. Then he had found out about the checks.

By bouncing seven of his company checks she had put RSK Petroleum Corporation in a bind. Six of them were small, so bouncing them was no big deal. But returning the seventh, the big one, was going to cause more trouble than he needed at that point in time.

Control your temper, he ordered himself. At the beach, Marcella had admitted making a first-day mistake. And he'd responded to her on a personal level. But when he realized it involved him professionally, his attitude had taken a turn for the worse. It's easy to say "It'll be all right" when it involves the other fellow, he surmised. When it hits home, well . . .

Brent spied Marcella as she stepped through the bank's glass front door, making her way toward the parking lot. Toward him.

Marcella stopped short. Leaning against his snow-white convertible, Brent waited. What was she going to say? The sight of his lazy stance added further despair. But he didn't appear angry. Moving away from the auto, he grinned slowly, then sauntered toward her. No, he looks like a cat stalking its prey, she surmised and dreaded the next moments.

"I ought to break your pretty little neck."

"You know," she said dully.

"I put two and two together."

"I'm sorry."

"Tell that to the Railroad Commission when they shut down my well," he said, brushing the arm of his lightweight tan suit.

"They wouldn't."

"They would. And if you're worth two cents as an oil-and-gas banker you'd know the law says they can close down a rig if a lease-payment check bounces."

The muscles of her face tensed with the realization. "I'll talk with the royalty owner."

"Save it. Nevill Rogers won't be interested." He turned his back, one hand on the car-door handle, then tilted his head to eye her with disgust. "I had one helluva time getting him to agree to lease the mineral rights in the first place. Now he'll think he was right all along, that I'm a fly-by-night oil operator."

"But—"

"By the way, Marcella, you should watch your mouth. This is a small town. You never know who you might be insulting. That 'birdbrain' who answered the telephone in my office happens to be my baby sister. She's running the office until my extremely capable secretary, who broke her collarbone in a car smashup, is back on her feet."

Yes, she had even insulted his family. "Oh Lord, I don't know what to say. What can I do to make it up to you?"

Brent hiked a brow at Marcella.

She eyed him suspiciously. The heel of his palm was resting on the top edge of the ragtop's door. She planted her clutch purse under her arm and stepped back on the parking-lot pavement. His fury was understandable. She had undermined his reputation by returning those checks. Not to mention what she had said about his sister. But surely he didn't mean to extract his pound of flesh by way of…a pound of flesh.

"I will not go to bed with you."

"What brought that on?" His eyes mocked her, and he moved closer, one hand capturing her elbow, the other grabbing her purse and tossing it onto the car seat. "But while we're on the subject, it's a tempting idea. I wouldn't play hard to get."

Defiantly, blue met green. Her heart beat wildly. "I'll bet you wouldn't."

"You're right about that. I'm interested. Just say the word."

"Don't hold your breath. I may never let you know."

"We'll see about that."

"You're not my type."

"We'll see about that," he repeated.

She didn't respond, merely bit her lip and looked away. While she had shied away from him in the beginning, she was now drawn to him. What was she going to do?

A sleek black car pulled up beside them. Marcella turned at the sound of an electric window being lowered. Sneed Goodman, smiling pleasantly, offered his nicely manicured hand to Brent.

"Brent! Nice to see you, Son."

He clasped the older man's hand. "How's it going, Pop?"

"Couldn't be better." Mr. Goodman waved at Marcella. "I see you've met Brent Coulter. Take good care of him, Marcella. He's a fine man."

She answered something, she wasn't sure what. Marcella couldn't understand the familiarity and respect Brent and her employer showed each other. After all, Brent was no longer married to Goodman's daughter. Didn't they harbor any animosity? Marcella supposed not, recalling how fast Sneed Goodman had sprung to RSK Petroleum's defense. The two men continued to chat for a minute, then the distinguished bank president said his adieus and drove away.

Her employer's presence had also called to mind her problem. She still owed Brent Coulter an apology. She faced him. He'd dug his hands into the pockets of his trousers, the action pleating up the jacket tail. And he was watching her intently.

Finally Marcella broke the silence with, "I'm truly sorry about the mix-up with your account. Like I told you last night, I made a mistake. I thought I was protecting the bank. I'm willing to rectify my error in any way professionally possible."

He accepted the apology offhandedly, as though there were now other things on his mind. Suddenly, unexpectedly, he asked, "Is your career the most important thing in your life?"

Marcella was taken aback for a moment. Her career was just about everything to her. She faced the pressures and the challenges with zeal. But from the look on Brent's face, she doubted that was what he wanted to hear.

"It's a living, that's all." Her statement wasn't a total fabrication.

The answer must have satisfied him; he smiled with warmth. Tilting her chin with a crooked finger, he winked an eye. "A few minutes ago, I was ready to tan your hide. But I can't stay upset with you. What do you say to my previous offer of friendship, until we understand more about each other?"

"I'd lo— I'd like that very much." She swallowed. "Brent, I'll telephone the royalty owner and the government people, too, and explain that your accounts are solvent, which they are, I've discovered. As for your sister, it was unkind of me to say what I did about her. I'm sure she's a lovely girl."

"I don't know how much good it'll do to call Nevill or the Railroad Commission. I'm going to be in one helluva bind with them, but as the saying goes, I'll cross that bridge when I come to it. And, yes, my sister is a lovely girl, who could benefit from your organizational abilities." Gallantly he brought Marcella's fingers to his lips, the warmth of his breath dancing across the skin of her knuckles. "Come on, let's have dinner... pal."

Brent waited for her answer. Cella was keeping a tight rein on her emotions, but she had responded with fire before having second thoughts the previous night. He had a niggling suspicion that someone had hurt her bad. Real bad. Obviously she needed to learn to trust him. And, to be honest, he wanted to know more about her before he got in over his head. Especially more about her attitude toward her career. Did it mean more than her personal life?

When she smiled, looped her arm through his and finally answered, "I'd like that very much," he was sailing on the wings of hope.

From that day on Marcella began to put her faith in Brent. He made no fast moves during their nightly dates—dates strictly limited to food experiences. To her confusion, Brent stalled each time she offered to fix dinner for him, as if he was hesitant to spend time in her home. Small-town fare left something to be desired in her estimation, she had discovered after they had visited the eating establishments, such as there were, in Port Merritt.

But she wasn't going to let that bother her.

Gentle, almost brotherly had been his good-night kisses. But she hadn't been unaware of the hungry look in his eyes when he thought she wasn't noticing.

Early Saturday afternoon he stopped by her house and asked if she was interested in an outing in the country. Marcella was delighted. Hastily she changed into a khaki skirt, oxford shirt and her worn Top-siders. She thought of dressing in something more...more, well, sexy. But she changed her mind. You don't need to appear sexy to a friend, she reasoned. Why she brushed her hair into lustrous waves and let it flow freely down her back, she didn't know.

As Brent's dust-covered Bronco rolled over a south Texas side road, Marcella scanned his solid, lean form, and gave mental appreciation to his rugged appearance. The sleeves of his faded denim shirt were rolled to just below the elbows; three unfastened buttons at the top gave her an arousing view of his rye-hued, hair-whorled chest. She gazed at his big square hands holding a thermos of coffee to his lips...capable hands with palms toughened from manual labor and with a manly network of veins across the tops. She shifted on the seat, thinking back to the feel of those fingers at the nape of her neck, on her cheek, touching her arm. No matter that she didn't trust her heart—she was a woman who responded to him instinctively. How much longer could she deny the desire she had for his hands to touch her?

Marcella was awfully afraid that her sentiments for him went beyond a fleeting attraction. And she was petrified that he wouldn't be able to return her feelings. There were too many unanswered questions, too many old heartaches that held a tight grip on her emotions. Jim had left her unable to trust completely. And, too, she suspected Brent harbored feelings for his former wife and he was starkly defensive about the institution of marriage. These things were not discussed, but never left her thoughts when Marcella was with, or away from, Brent. So many matters of the heart were yet to be discovered. And until then keep it light, she cautioned herself.

The country music on the truck radio changed to a Spanish broadcast. "Find something else, will you, hon," he requested.

Turning the dial, she asked, "Do you like classical music?"

"Sure. As long as George Jones sings it."

"Heretic."

"Stuffed shirt," he countered. "And I do love the way you stuff your shirt."

He stuffed his shirt nicely, too. Everything about him was oversize and lean. Even his possessions were massive, such as his gentle Doberman pinscher, who had joined them for their outing. As if the dog in the back seat had read her mind, Fred dropped her chin onto Marcella's shoulder.

The animal's long pink tongue raked her jaw. She twitched and pushed at the dog's muzzle. "Stop that Fredi!" Marcella couldn't bring herself to call a female dog by a masculine appellation. "You're giving me the willies."

Puppy eyes watched her sorrowfully.

"Don't like my dog, huh?"

"I adore your dog. I just don't like to be licked." In conciliation Marcella scratched a floppy ear. "I thought Dobermans were supposed to have short pointy ears."

"Only if they're cropped." Brent whipped his black-rimmed aviator sunglasses from the bridge of his nose and placed them on the dashboard. His look was rather abashed. "I didn't have the heart to put her through it."

"Big ol' softie," she said with a grin as she twisted to face him. "Don't you think it's about time you told me where we're going?"

"Okay, if you insist." A lingering grin pulled at his cheek as he rested a wrist on the steering wheel. "I want you to see my baby."

"Brent Coulter! You never mentioned you have a child."

"Whoa! It's not like that." He maneuvered the vehicle around a bend in the mesquite- and palm-lined road, then braked the truck to a halt off the road. "There she is." His finger pointed straight ahead. "My baby: the Rollins exploratory."

Marcella faced forward. A cold chill ran the length of her spine, and she sucked in her breath sharply. The vicious nightmare of childhood loomed before her— an obelisk testament to loss in the form of foreboding iron and steel; killing pipes and cables.

"What's the matter?" Brent asked in a tone of concern, his hand settling over her frozen fingers.

Marcella flinched from the unexpected action. "Nothing," she replied.

Brent got out of the Bronco, turned, and extended both arms to help her from the high seat. "Come on. The tool pusher's expecting us. You'll get a grand tour of the rig floor."

Her voice was weak, hollow. "No."

"Hey, my baby won't bite you." He tugged at her hands. "I'm saving that honor for myself. Whoa, sorry there. Forgot myself for a minute, pal."

It took all her resources of strength to alight from the vehicle; she wasn't able to respond to his joking. Marcella stood stock-still as he went around to the tailgate and let the dog out.

In her professional life she had been able to divorce herself from the physical existence of a drilling rig. Paper and figures were merely paper and figures.

To come face-to-face with this baneful reality left her rigid. This was all too real. And she would not set foot on that hulking assassin.

From the rig floor a man—the driller, she guessed—shouted orders over the drone of a powerful motor and the piercing clang of pipe and chain. Seeking relief, her field of vision swept to a metal building that stood yards from the rig. A small native-rock house—a possible refuge?—was situated several furlongs behind the metal building.

"Brent, I'm feeling a little light-headed," she said. "Is there any place where I might freshen up?"

A look of genuine hurt crossed his face. "Well, uh, sure. That cabin over there is for my use—it was part of the leasing agreement I made with Rogers. It's my personal home-away-from-home. No one who values his job would dare enter without knocking. You'll have plenty of privacy."

She murmured, "Thanks," as he escorted her to the old house. Forcing thoughts of the rig from her mind, she concentrated on the interior. The dwelling had only one room and was filled with rather dilapidated country-style furnishings. Piles of drilling logs and reports were scattered over slipcovered chairs, a divan-style sofa and cigarette-charred tables. An iron bed with a tattered quilt sat along one wall.

Brent dropped a stack of papers to the floor, his hand indicating the sofa. "Sit down, Cella. I'll get you a cool cloth and a 7-Up."

Planting her elbows on her knees and leaning her forehead against her knuckles, she chewed her upper lip. Brent returned, hunkering down beside her. He coaxed her to sip the soft drink and he bathed her face as if she were a child. Gradually she began to feel a measure of rationality.

"Think you can tell me what's the problem?"

Tears moistened her lashes as she closed her eyelids. She felt an overwhelming need to talk about the accident. Never before had she spoken candidly about it.

"When I was ten my father was k-killed on an oil rig." She wiped her hand under her nostrils. "That infernal west Texas wind gusted up. Dammit all!" Her thin shoulders shook as she buried her face in her hands. "Daddy... He... Oh, God rest his soul.... A piece of pipe fell out of the rack. It...fell to the rig floor and cr-crushed his skull."

"Sweet mercies, I shouldn't have brought you out here." He slid onto the seat, enveloping her in his comforting arms, and rocked her gently. His fingers combed the heavy fall of black hair from her cheek. "Cella, I'm sorry."

"There's no need to be sorry. It wasn't your fault." She swallowed the lump in her throat, picking up the soft-drink bottle. "I saw it happen."

He recoiled. "What in the name of Pete were you doing near an oil rig!"

"Daddy had been in a rig accident not too long before that. We were dirt poor from medical expenses and the wages he'd lost. I suppose the tool pusher felt sorry for us—he let Daddy park our house trailer on the lease." She set the bottle aside, suddenly remembering the good times. "I liked being out there. I'd fix sandwiches and coffee for the men coming off crew change.

"The other roughnecks and the driller were Daddy's poker-playing pals, and they'd congregate in our trailer." She laughed shallowly. "I've popped a mountain of long-neck beer tops in my day."

"Where was your mother during all of this?"

"I never knew my mother."

"What happened to you after... after your father passed away?"

"Oh, a couple of the roughnecks wanted to take me into their homes, but the courts looked down their noses at—in the judge's opinion—oil-patch trash. He decided that I'd be better off under the state's protection. I—" she paused "—I existed in an orphanage until I was old enough to take care of myself."

"I never guessed," he said slowly.

"I'll never forget those miserable years. I kept crying for my daddy to come and get me. Once I accepted the fact that he was dead, I started dreaming my dreams of the day I'd be out of that place."

Expressing her deep-seated resentment gave Marcella the courage to verbalize at last her inner torment. "In all honesty, I guess I blamed my father for what happened, for not loving me enough to turn his back on the dangers of his job. Where was I lacking? What had I done that made him not love me enough to give it up?'' Her control folded like a house of cards, sobs racking her body. ''I miss him so much,'' she moaned disjointedly. ''I get scared sometimes. I don't have anyone.''

''You have me,'' Brent said softly. Holding her closely, he yearned to pour his storehouse of strength into her frail, anguished body.

For several minutes he held her. Over and over in his mind he rehashed her confession. He knew her well enough to know that her words hadn't come easy for her. She hadn't had much happiness in her life. He wanted her to be happy.

He thought of his own background. Even though the Coulters had been rich one year, poor the next, his people had always had a strong nucleus of familial ties. And abruptly he realized how little money matters for happiness. Even when the Coulter clan had been eating beans they had laughed, loved and been there for each other in times of troubles. That's what he would be for Cella.

''You have me,'' he repeated.

Marcella took a quivering breath of air, glancing up at him warily. ''Don't say something you don't mean.''

''Don't create your own problems. I'm your friend. Remember?''

''Yes. My friend.'' She faced the window. ''You must think I'm a basket case.''

''No, Cella, I think you're beautiful.'' He tweaked her nose, trying to make light of the situation and seeking to ease her troubled mind. ''Especially with a schnoz that Rudolph would be proud of.'' After wiping the last tear from her cheek with his thumb, he held her face between his palms. "Feel better now?"

"Yes. You have an amazing ability to make me feel better."

"That shouldn't surprise you. We were meant to be, Cella."

Time stood still for Marcella as she gazed into Brent's eyes and saw all that was there. She slowly became aware of his solid body pressed oh, so near to hers, and of his breath caressing her cheeks and senses. Her palms grazed the soft chambray of his shirt, and she savored the scent of soap and after-shave and man.

"Kiss me," she said in a low voice.

"Oh, baby...."

Tilting his head to hers, Brent tenderly grasped her hair. His eyes were half-closed with the fire of longing. His lips parted fractionally, and hers answered in kind. Marcella felt a certain intensity to his body as the warmth of his mouth became one with hers, and he murmured her name. As if they had been created for each other, the stroke of his velvet tongue on her lips and in the inner secrets of her mouth seemed natural and right. She savored the gentle exploration, sighing at the wonder of it, marveling at its drugging pleasure. Suddenly with an ardency she never realized she possessed, her tongue twined with his and she deepened the embrace. He gasped as though he had been jolted. Moving even closer, she bonded her body tightly to his powerful frame.

Abruptly a knock sounded against the front door, bringing Marcella back to her senses. She pulled away from Brent. Self-consciously straightening her hair, she watched him unfold his legs, stride across the room and throw the door open.

"What's up?" he asked a diminutive russet-haired man.

"Coulter, the tool pusher needs to see you in his shack."

"Well, come in for a minute, Jerry. There's someone I want you to meet." After quick introductions he winked at Marcella. "Keep Cella company, buddy, till I can get back."

"Aye, aye, cap'n."

In retrospect Marcella was thankful for the interruption. Jerry Hagen had unknowingly rescued her from the dangers of a moment of weakness when her desire had overruled her head.

Keeping that in mind, Marcella turned her attention to the homely geologist. Jerry was easy to like, she decided as she watched him search through an ancient Kelvinator that chugged in the corner and then prepare a pot of coffee. He had an earnestness that was appealing. He liked antiques, she learned. Classical music, too. To keep her mind off Brent—and that hulking menace of an oil rig—she kept up an idle conversation with Jerry. It was odd, she thought, that before she had met Brent, Jerry would have seemed the ideal man for her. Now her ideals ran to— Marcella, don't even think like that, she warned herself.

Jerry blew the coffee's steam, observing her over the rim of a chipped cup. "I understand you're vice president of Goodman National."

With a paper napkin she rubbed a layer of dust from the table. "Yes, I am."

He leaned back in his chair. "Tell me, Marcella, do you know much about the oil business? You know, as it relates to financing."

"Yes, of course," she replied. "I worked in the oil-and-gas department of a bank in Houston for several years before coming to Goodman National. Why do you ask?"

"Know anything about reading a drilling report?"

"Yes."

"Good. I was wondering if I might ask you to do something. Confidentially, of course. Would you take a look at some data from the Rollins One and tell me what you think the financial prospects might be?"

She didn't like this line of conversation. If the past six days had taught her anything, it was that Brent's fierce pride wouldn't allow her to interfere in his business dealings.

"I conduct business at Goodman National, Jerry."

"Since you and Brent are friends, would you make an exception this time?"

She regarded him warily. To discuss business outside the bank went against her personal credo, but Jerry seemed earnest in his concern for RSK. Should she make a one-time exception?

"Does Brent know you're asking me to read the report?"

"No," Jerry answered after a short gap in time. "There's something you need to know about Brent Coulter. He needs money, bad, to complete this well. He's having trouble with the bank that loaned him start-up funds. And, well, his pride won't let him go to Sneed Goodman and ask for a loan. I can't let all the money he's invested go down the drain! Would you take a look and give me your honest opinion?''

She ached to inquire if Brent's reticence was associated with his feelings for Sneed's daughter, but knew that question was between her and Brent. Instead she asked, ''Are you asking me for a loan, Mr. Hagen?''

''No, Ms. Parker, I'm asking you for an opinion.''

''I won't go behind Brent's back.''

He offered her a folder. ''Marcella, I'm asking you for an opinion, nothing more. I've got to find a way to help RSK Petroleum through this rough spot. You won't be doing anything behind Brent's back but maybe advising me on how I can help him.''

More than anything Marcella wanted to help the wildcatter, as his employee wanted to help him. Would it be unfair to Brent to merely look over the material?

''All right. But understand one thing: I'll give you my honest opinion.'' Reluctantly she took the document.

''What do you think?'' Jerry asked a short while later.

''What's the monetary history on this project?''

The geologist explained the start-up financing for the Rollins Field. Marcella inhaled sharply as she mentally calculated total capital outlay. During boom times, when petroleum drilling was at its zenith, the figures would not have been outlandish. But those days were over. Low crude prices and the glut of world oil made wildcatting a chancy venture. At best.

But someway, somehow, she had to find a way to help Brent. How, she didn't know. Book value wasn't that impressive; RSK was already overextended on the project. Well completion would take a great deal of money, in the mid-to-high six figures. And even then there were no absolute guarantees that it would become a high-yield well. One of her customers was operating a tract in this vicinity of south Texas, she recalled. Production was low on that discovery well, averaging about fifty barrels a day.

Jerry concluded his mini-speech and looked at Marcella expectantly. She hesitated a minute to compose the words she would use when she told him the truth.

Brent wiped beads of sweat from his brow as he approached the cabin. He was eager to return to Marcella, although not to take up where they'd left off. It was neither the time nor the place for the act of love. Feeling guilty, he realized how close he'd been to taking advantage of her vulnerability. And he didn't like that in himself. She was beginning to mean the world to him, was beginning to occupy a niche in his heart. When they made love he wanted it to be special, something they would both remember with pleasure. Not in a setting that caused so many hurtful memories for Marcella.

Brent stopped in his tracks when he heard her voice through a crack in the window.

"I wouldn't loan ten cents to this venture."

"Not even for Brent? Even if it means this well'll have to be abandoned?"

"Let me explain something to you, Jerry. I never mix business with pleasure. Bankers have a responsibility to investors and to depositors. Loans are extended with the promise of return on investment. This project is iffy, to say the least. If Brent Coulter wants a loan, he'll have to ask Mr. Goodman. But if it ever comes up in a Loan Committee meeting, I can guarantee you that I'll vote against it."

"You're a heartless woman, Marcella."

"When it comes to business, yes." She paused. "Now if you'll excuse me, I think I need a breath of air."

"Is that your last word?"

"Yes."

"Even if Brent asked you himself?"

Anger slammed through Brent. He ought to charge in there and break Jerry's jaw! Then shake the living daylights out of Marcella for sticking her nose into his affairs, he seethed. He shot away from the ego-crushing conversation. Damn them to hell!

He hadn't asked her for anything. He hadn't asked anything from anybody. He had seen his father snivel and beg in the oil business when times were tough. Brent had made a pledge to himself a long time earlier that he would never be in the same situation. He wouldn't scrape down to her—or to Sneed!—even if it meant financial ruin.

"After tonight I'm finished with you, Marcella. But by God, tonight's mine," he muttered as he stalked away.

## Chapter Four

Accompanied by Brent's Doberman, Marcella explored the flat terrain away from the drilling rig, hoping to find solutions within herself. Wrenching memories of her childhood were filed into the recesses of her brain. Eighteen years of practice had taught her the futility of dwelling on self-pity.

She couldn't bring herself to return to the cabin. Not yet. Instead she concentrated on the simple pleasures of communing with nature. The air, untouched by city pollution, eased her tensions.

When Fredi wasn't chasing jackrabbits through the buffalo grass or pestering a bewildered armadillo, the dog ran circles around thin-trunked palm trees and spiny, white-budded mesquites—and Marcella, who was buoyed by the dog's carefree spirit. Watching the canine flatten herself in a patch of bluebonnets to sniff the earth, Marcella laughed warmly.

Fredi had much the same spirit as her master. They were both big and scary until she got to know them, but gentle and affectionate after the beginning.

Oh, Brent! What am I going to do about you? she wondered, finding no easy answers, no simple solutions. Had she gotten in too deeply with him? Should she tell him about her conversation with Jerry Hagen? What could she do to help Brent's financially troubled corporation?

Marcella knew Brent had faith in himself and his endeavors and that he was driven to succeed in his ventures. It took grit to establish an oil exploration company during troubled economic times, and she respected his ambition. But was that enough? If she were to become the kind of friend Brent would allow into his confidence, she needed to know more about other facets of his life. But one thing she understood: Brent was not the type of man to accept unasked-for help.

And she had to be honest with him. To keep Jerry's conversation a secret would be unpardonable.

The cloak of dust was settling as she and Fredi hiked back up the dirt road leading to the Rollins One. Averting her eyes from the string of harsh lights outlining the drilling rig, Marcella hugged her arms against the chill in her bones. *Don't think about that monstrosity.*

Again she thought of Brent. Somehow she had to convince him to allow her to use her professional abilities to his benefit. That's what friends were for, and she would make Brent accept that.

The dog, sensing her anxieties, looked up with soulful eyes. Forcing a smile, Marcella patted the sleek head. "Don't worry, Fredi, everything's going to be okay." The Doberman took off in a run, lumbering over to the shack and leaving Marcella to open the weathered front door.

Quiet in the one-room cabin was all too pervasive, darkness all too prevalent. The interior was lit only by the orange glow of a cigarette, its tip smoldering brighter, then ebbing. Moving forward, she heard someone blow a heavy cloud of smoke. "Brent?"

At the same moment the room was bathed in muted hues from a lamp. Half lying, half sitting, Brent reclined shirtless, braced by his elbows atop the bed's multicolored quilt. His long legs were crossed and extended over the edge of the iron bed. The look in his eyes was as smoky as the ribbons of vapor curling toward the ceiling.

"Where've you been, baby?" he asked in a tone far too husky to be normal as he twisted his upper body to adroitly grind the cigarette stub into an ashtray.

"I needed some air."

When she entered the room, which she noticed had been straightened to a semblance of order, her heart turned over with apprehension. Earlier she had led him to believe she would acquiesce to passion. Apparently he hadn't forgotten—the bedside table held a galvanized pail filled with brown beer bottles and a stubby candle set in an empty aluminum can. Her feet stopped moving a few steps from him.

"I—I didn't know you smoked," she remarked, for lack of anything better to say.

"Only when the occasion calls for it." Leaning forward, he extended his hand. "Come here."

As if in a daze she complied, sitting down on the edge of the bed. "Brent, about this afternoon—"

"Are you scared of me?"

"A little." She was more scared of herself than of Brent; simply being with him weakened her willpower to keep friendship the extent of their relationship.

"That makes two of us." He brushed one hand along her forearm and reached for a book of matches with the other. "You light the candle, and I'll put on a little mood music."

With shaking fingers she grasped the matchbook and did as he bade, while Brent reached to push a cassette into a portable tape deck. The room was filled with the sound of a sweet, provocative classical melody.

He brought her wrist close to his lips, blowing out the flame of the match she still held. "Like the music?"

"Yes," she answered weakly.

"Thank Jerry next time you see him," he said in a strangely unreadable voice. "Sorry there's no champagne. Hope you won't mind making do with a lesser evil."

In a move that left her further hypnotized, he lightly ran his lips along the inside of her wrist, her forearm. A mélange of sensations danced in her being, and as if weightless, her head swayed backward, her eyelids closing. She heard the flick of the light switch, sensed rather than saw the sudden darkness.

Reaching for her, his fingers tightened around her upper arms as he pulled her to him. Nestled between his legs, with her body covering his, she was heady with excitement. As if they had minds of their own, her palms curved over his shoulders, her nails working his muscled flesh. His mouth met hers in a fervent kiss that left her breathless and begging for more.

"God, how I want you," he whispered raggedly, almost roughly.

The tremor of his words, the feel of his body, the musky scent of his skin…everything about Brent was sending her on a thrilling sensory journey. The erratic beat of her heart pulsed in her neck as the gentle caress of his lips touched her throat, his mustache brushing, tempting her sensitive skin.

"I need you," he murmured.

Suddenly there was no one in the world but the two of them. She opened her eyes, and his gaze spoke the language of desire, never faltering from hers. Smoothly he eased away her blouse buttons. His thumb sensuously caressed one hardened peak.

"Oh, Brent." She surrendered as his teeth nibbled her earlobe, sending an added flush of heat through every cell in her body.

"I'm going to make love to you till—"

Abruptly Brent lapsed into silence, those two little words bringing him to his senses. If they continued it wouldn't be making love, it would be having sex. There was no denying he craved the woman, but it would be wrong to take her in a fit of anger.

He realized his earlier motivations to avenge his fury by taking Marcella had lacked maturity. Though he knew they weren't right for each other, he respected her, and himself, too much to make a mockery out of the strong feelings he'd once held for her.

"What's wrong?" she asked, moving away from him.

He switched on the light once more. "We'd better start back for Port Merritt."

Something was very amiss, Marcella realized. Brent's face was a stone mask, unreadable and every line of his body taut.

She caught his arm, and he pulled it back to his side. "There's something I need to tell you before we leave, Brent."

"Save it."

"I won't." Trembling, she began to button her blouse. "Jerry Hagen asked for financial advice about your drilling rig."

"I heard. Your little speech about the worth of this property was quite enlightening, Marcella."

The heavy weight of embarrassment sank through her as she realized how her words must have sounded. "Oh, Brent, I didn't mean—"

"I learned more about you than I ever wanted to know when you were playing lady banker with the hired help, Ms. Parker."

"I said what I did in order to protect you."

"Your brand of protection—" he jumped to his feet and charged across the room "—I can do without."

"Won't you let me explain?"

He studied the darkness outside the now-closed window, then whipped back to observe her. Sadness, disillusionment and stark pain were reflected in his eyes.

"There's nothing to explain. I heard it with my own ears."

Further discussion on the subject would be a waste of time, Marcella realized. Brent needed time to get over his anger before he would be rational enough to listen. In the meantime she'd try to gather what little composure she had left. "I'll wait outside."

"An idle mind is the devil's workshop" was instilled in Marcella long ago by a dormitory matron at the orphanage. And in the two days since the ill-fated trip to the Rollins Field, she had kept herself busy, although it hadn't been easy.

Keeping occupied at the bank had been no problem. But at home, how much cooking and cleaning could she do just to keep Brent Coulter from dominating her thoughts? The larder was overstocked, the freezer was filled with home-prepared food to the point of not closing and—heaven forbid!—the floors could be eaten from.

She missed Brent. How she regretted her conversation with Jerry Hagen. If only she had refused his request to look over those drilling reports.... She supposed helping Brent was completely out of the question. Obviously he wanted nothing more to do with her; he'd pointedly ignored her since he'd made a cursory apology when he left her on her doorstep after they had returned from the Rollins Field. But be that as it may, she still wanted to gain his trust. She was, after all, the officer in charge of his accounts at Goodman National. Who was she trying to kid? She had a personal interest in Brent that she had no intention of squelching. If the right opportunity came along, she intended to be his friend once more. And her patience with his absence was just about wearing thin.

Monday evening arrived. She could hear voices, muffled male and female voices, from Brent's side of the house. Well, it was his prerogative to entertain whoever he pleased, but she felt an undeniable twinge of jealousy.

In a huff she parked herself on the sofa and picked up the crewel wall hanging that she'd begun the past Sunday. After pricking her finger she gave up on embroidery. She thumbed through the TV program booklet, then placed it neatly on the rosewood coffee table. She could sit around moping, but not forever.

And then his side of the duplex was quiet. Suddenly a timid knock sounded against the front door. "Well, that can't be Brent," she muttered dryly. "If he wanted in, he'd bang the door down."

On the stoop was a young woman, hand raised to knock again.

"Hi, I'm Debbie Coulter, Brent's sister." The girl smiled, displaying an elfin grin. Freckles dotted her nose, and her hair was a riot of light brown curls. "I've been visiting my brother, and I just wanted to stop by and introduce myself." She went on in a rush, "May I come in?"

Marcella suddenly felt marvelous. Brent had been entertaining his sister! Of course Debbie could come in, and Marcella made welcoming social banter. How nice to meet you. Would she have a cup of tea? No. A glass of cola? Yes.

Perhaps this was the entrée Marcella needed to mend fences with Brent.

Once seated on the sofa Debbie took a swallow of the soft drink. "Do you remember me? You called the office one day and I answered the phone."

"Um, yes, I do," Marcella answered, remembering quite well the repercussions of that telephone conversation. She sat down on the wing chair next to the sofa. "Does Brent know you're over here?"

"I dunno. Probably not."

Marcella sensed trouble. But she was in it this far...and she hoped for the best. She surveyed the girl, who didn't look at all like her brother. "I must admit, you're not as I pictured."

The pixie giggled. "I'll bet you expected me to be tall and sandy haired like Brent." Marcella nodded. "Everybody does until they meet Mom and Dad. I take after our father. Brent favors Mom—except he's sorta nearsighted and a southpaw like Dad. Everyone calls them Mutt and Jeff—not Brent and Mom—I mean my parents. Only Mom's the Jeff and Dad's the Mutt. Now you know all about us." Debbie grinned, flashing a beautiful set of even white teeth much like her brother's. "And Brent's told me all about you."

"Really?" Marcella asked incredulously. After the past Saturday she'd figured he had forgotten her completely.

"Oh, yes. I think he's kinda mad at you right now, though, 'cause every time I bring up your name, he tells me to find something else to do. But don't worry," she hastened to add, "he always gets glad just like he gets mad."

"Does he?"

"Oh, yes. Lefty—" she curled her fingers over her mouth "—oops, I mean, Brent. He always gets angry when I call him Lefty. He has a bad temper, in case you haven't noticed."

"He has more than his share of good traits, too."

"It's super to hear you say that, Marcella." Debbie's voice took on a worshipful quality. "He's a really special guy. Sometimes he gets aggravated at me, but I guess that's to be expected since he's *ages* older than I am."

Marcella chuckled inwardly, envisioning his youth and vitality. "Debbie, isn't he thirty?"

"Yes," she strung out. "But he's pretty good-looking for an older guy, don't you think?"

"He's very handsome... for an old timer."

"I'm seventeen," Debbie explained. "This is my senior year in high school, and I'm working mornings and evenings for RSK through the distributive education department of my school." She dropped her chin, coloring slightly. "That's why I didn't answer the telephone when you called back the other day. I was in class."

Marcella was further embarrassed by her unthinking remarks the previous week to Brent.

"Do you like my brother—I mean, do you like him a lot?"

"Very much."

"Are you mad at him, Marcella?"

The topic was best dropped. "Would you like a cookie?"

"No, thank you." Debbie placed her hands primly on her lap. With irises as green as her brother's she observed Marcella. "Brent says you're very good at your job."

"That was kind of him."

"He said I could learn a lot from you."

"Debbie, I'm sure I couldn't teach you a thing."

"Golly, don't be modest. Brent doesn't sing praises he doesn't mean." Debbie chewed her lower lip, a gesture that clearly said she had more on her mind. "I need to ask a favor of you."

"In what way?"

"I have to work in Brent's office all by myself until his secretary Crickett gets back on her feet. She was in a car wreck, in case you didn't know." Debbie's childlike features held an impassioned plea. "Would you help me? I can't seem to get my act together. And I will *never* forget how Brent fussed at me about your telephone call!"

Marcella was hesitant to answer. She liked Brent's sister. A great deal. Debbie reminded Marcella of herself when she had started out in the business world. Eager, green and with a lot to learn. But if she agreed to train her, how would Brent feel about it?

"Please, Marcella. For the rest of this week, anyway. I'll be happy to pay you."

How could she say no? Well, to the money she would. She wanted to help the girl...and her brother. Deep inside, Marcella needed to be needed. Further, she had a natural curiosity about the inner workings of RSK Petroleum Corporation. And it would be the perfect opportunity to find out how she could help Brent with his financial troubles.

She capitulated and extended her hand. "I'll be happy to help you, Debbie. Starting tomorrow evening and through Friday. And in payment you can show me around Port Merritt. Agreed?"

"You've got a deal." Debbie pumped Marcella's hand, then inquired hopefully, "Will you be able to come in to the office and help me?"

"If your brother isn't too opposed—yes!"

"Oh, don't worry about Brent. I'll handle him." His sister took another quick swallow of cola, then set the glass on the wooden edge of the coffee table.

Marcella extracted a pad of paper and a pen from a table drawer, passing them to the girl while instructing her to take notes. To begin, she dictated a work schedule, and Debbie took arduous notations. Surreptitiously Marcella grabbed a napkin, moved the glass of cola to a coaster and wiped the ring of moisture from the table. Then she began a training session on business-telephone technique.

As Debbie was carefully dotting the final *i* and crossing the last *t* on the paper, a loud bang followed by three staccato rings of the doorbell bounced off the walls.

That *had* to be Brent!

Marcella barely opened the door when he stomped into her living room, pointing a finger at his sister. "Debra Coulter, I escorted you to your car—I made sure you were safe and sound. And what did I hear when I'm trying to read the newspaper? I'll tell you what I heard—your voice through the wall!"

"I could've told you that, Lef—Brent, just by the way you barged in here."

Marcella crossed her arms over her chest, regarding the ruggedly featured man wearing horn-rimmed glasses. Her attention drifted away from the situation she should have been paying attention to. He'd never worn glasses in her presence. They looked marvelous on him! She felt a thudding in her heart; his presence did that to her. He wore jogging shorts that exposed his well-toned thighs and calves to their best advantage, and his light green polo shirt heightened the brilliance of his eyes, even behind those glasses. What was the matter with her? How he appeared was of no importance at the present!

"Now listen here, Mr. Coulter. You can do as you please in your own house, but I won't have you charging in here and bothering my guest."

"It's all right, Marcella. I'm not scared of him." Debbie crossed her legs, swinging one foot saucily, and leaned back against the sofa. "Brent, aren't you going to say hello to Marcella?"

An encounter with Marcella was the last thing Brent could handle. She had been in his thoughts, in his fantasies since the moment he had left her at her door on Saturday night. The hurt within him had cooled with the passing of time. His actions that day at the rig had been a clear-cut case of overreacting. Seeing her again, he was almost willing to say to hell with everything, to throw her over his shoulder and carry her away. Almost willing.

Cella's attitude, with the exception of her banker persona, reeked of a wedding ring and a lifetime commitment. But so had Vicky's, at least before the ink was dry on the marriage license. And the mere thought of his ex-wife renewed his convictions to remain unattached. Squaring his shoulders, he slowly turned to face Cella. His heart stopped. She needed to be told how gorgeous she was in those white slacks and that petal-pink pullover top. God, she was beautiful!

He forced an evenness into his tone. "Hello, Marcella."

To her, his voice held a gentle roughness, rolling through her as a palliative to past disagreements. Whether he were angry, happy, or whatever his frame of mind, she had missed his presence, she thought sadly. This man was one hundred eighty degrees wrong for her, but . . . she still felt a need to help him and his company.

"Hello, Brent." A tiny smile touched the corners of her mouth. "Would you like to sit down?"

He turned back to Debbie. "Are you leaving with me?"

"No."

"Figures." Eyeing Marcella, he raked his fingers through his shock of hair. "Then I have no choice but to stay and see what you're up to, Debra." He dropped into a club chair, his mammoth body dwarfing the small frame. Rubbing the back of his neck, he squinted at his sister. "What *are* you doing over here?"

"I wanted to meet Marcella. Guess what! She's agreed to help me in the office."

"Not no, but hell no!" he roared. Leaning forward, he pounded a fist on his knee. "I absolutely forbid it."

"Why?" Debbie asked innocently.

"She knows why."

"But you said she's smart, and you said I could learn a thing or two from her."

"Debra, you talk too much."

The girl glanced at him knowingly. "You said she's pretty, too."

Brent fidgeted. "I, uh, I imagine she knows that."

"You also told me that you wanted to get to know Marcella better."

"I was drunk."

"You were not! And what better way to get to know her than to have her right there in the office with us. Isn't that right, Marcella?"

"Debbie," Marcella replied, disquieted, "you're putting me on the spot."

"Listen here, Debra—" he pulled out his words for clear understanding "—when I need your advice, you'll be the first to know." He whipped off his horn-rimmed glasses, glaring at Marcella. "I don't need *her* for anything."

Tension crackled in the air as she met his wrathful gaze with one of her own. Marcella was livid. She had expected his reaction to Debbie's news, but she hadn't expected the intensity of her own reaction. He was making too big a deal of his anger over her innocent talk with Jerry Hagen. And by gosh, she had agreed to help Debbie, and she wasn't going to back down. This was a matter of principle.

"Let's go, Debbie," Brent said as he started to rise.

Arms swinging at her sides, Marcella marched over to his chair before he could get up—her best vantage point since, standing, he was a good foot taller than she—and looked daggers at him. She pushed him back with all the force she could garner.

"Sit down," she commanded tersely. Refusing to break visual contact with him, she asked, "Debbie, do you want me to help you?"

"Oh, yes, ma'am."

Storm clouds of fury blackened his face. "I'm the boss at RSK, and I say no."

"You don't want my help—fine! For your information, I'm not interested in helping you," Marcella prevaricated. "But put this in your pipe and smoke it: I'm not offering my services to you, Brent Coulter. I'm offering my assistance to your sister. Now, are you willing to let me help her or not?"

Brent grabbed the chair arms, squeezing the stuffings with all his might. He didn't want to give in; it was a point of pride. And personal freedom. Under any other circumstances he would have told Marcella Parker just what to do with her offer of help.

But his sister was sitting not five feet from him, expecting her older brother to behave in a manner befitting an elder. He had not behaved like an adult. Marcella had that effect on him, damn her. Well, if you can't beat them, join them, he figured. He couldn't let his sister down.

Turning her attention to Marcella, he sank back against the cushion. Her display of spunk appealed to him. A lot of things about her appealed to him. And a couple of things didn't. How was he going to avoid her at RSK? Someway, somehow, he would find the strength to keep his hands off her.

"All right, Ms. Parker, you win."

What was she getting herself into? Marcella asked herself. Being in close quarters, would she be able to quell her attraction to Brent Coulter? While the battle had been won, she was awfully afraid that she was well on her way to losing the war.

## Chapter Five

Friday evening, at the modest headquarters of RSK Petroleum Corporation, Marcella avoided eye contact with Brent as she double-checked Debbie's general ledger entries. But her mind wasn't on debits and credits. Rather, curiosity about what made Brent tick and about the company that he had founded filled her consciousness. Among other things...

She remembered the good times they had shared—tender moments, precious memories to cherish. Such thoughts were hazardous to her emotional well-being, made her yearn to loosen the belt of self-protection.

Friendship was out of the question. The previous Saturday night had disproved any hopes for platonic companionship. And since then Brent had ignored her during the nightly two-hour periods she had set aside to assist his sister. Clearly he didn't want Marcella's trust or help. Yet the fact that he allowed her full access to his financial records indicated a great deal of faith.

Brent worked tirelessly, Marcella surmised. Drilling continued round the clock and nothing slipped past his sharp eyes. His employees revered him and his decisions. Such blind devotion and loyalty were not a happenstance.

Working at RSK had a positive effect on Marcella. She was beginning to believe that the Rollins One would be a high-yield producer, deserving of Brent's stalwart visions. Yet it would take a lot of money to reach the reserves.

From her presence in his office, Marcella had a lead on a solution to Brent's cash flow problems. She had been waiting for the right moment, and then she'd intended to ask him about it. But her time had almost run out.

She stole a glance at him when Debbie asked, "Are you finished proofreading that contract, Brent?"

"Not quite, Debra. But it's looking good."

Marcella's resolve to ignore Brent Coulter was showing definite signs of a crack. Dressed in tan trousers and a continental-cut shirt, Brent leaned back in his high-back chair, his crossed feet propped on his desk, and was reading the contract. His hair was slightly mussed; reading glasses had slid halfway down his straight nose; the first signs of a five-o'clock shadow traced his strong jaw.

If he was any other man, his stance might have been considered too relaxed, perhaps idle. But Marcella knew from being in the office with him that Brent Coulter could accomplish more work with his feet propped up than most other males could when they hugged a desk.

The sight of his big-boned frame, the sound of his husky drawl and the manly scent of his herbal aftershave had gotten to her, Marcella admitted to herself as she closed the general ledger. "Debbie," she said, "the figures all check."

"Oh, super!"

"You've come a long way in the past few days," Marcella continued. "So from now on you're on your own. You don't need my help." Marcella stood and walked over to file the ledger. "I'll be leaving now."

Debbie gushed her gratitude for Marcella's instructions.

"Debra," Brent put in, "this contract is ready to go. Be a good egg and run it by the post office, please."

"Okay." She turned to Marcella. "Wanna go with me? I'll take you on a tour of Port Merritt afterward."

Marcella opened her mouth to accept, but Brent cut in. "Don't leave right yet, Cella. Stay a few minutes."

Debbie, obviously pleased that her brother wanted a few minutes alone with Marcella, smiled from ear to ear. "Aw, go on and stay, Marcella. You can go with me anytime."

"All right," Marcella acquiesced, not needing Debbie's prompting. Lead by the heart, Marcella turned to Brent. "I'll stay."

His sister departed, lightning fast.

"You've done a great job with Debbie, Cella. I want you to know that I appreciate what you've done for her...and for RSK. We'll miss you."

"Thank you," she replied softly.

"Come sit by me," he commanded softly. "Please."

Wanting to be nearer and happy for the chance, she glided over to him and leaned a hip against his desk.

"Your patience with my sister amazes me," he continued.

Beautifully arched brows quirked. "Patience with Debbie? That's the easiest thing in the world. She sort of reminds me of myself at that age."

"But she's a chatterbox and you're not."

"She wants to learn." Marcella grabbed the toe of his shoe, shaking it lightly. "Mostly to please you."

"Is that so bad? Wanting to please me?"

"I wouldn't count it as a deadly sin."

"Would you ever consider pleasing me?" he asked quietly.

Don't let him twist this conversation, she warned herself. Lurching away from his desk, she turned her back to him and began to clear her desk.

Brent watched her. He wouldn't mind pleasing her.... Sweet mercies, he was going crazy thinking of the ways he wanted to please her. This line of thinking was going to land him in trouble, trouble known as a long-term commitment. *Ease up, Coulter.* Why didn't he quit lying to himself? He was lonely, and he needed Cella in his life. But she was being quiet, too quiet. He had pushed her too far with the "pleasing" angle, he realized regretfully.

"Forget I asked that." He rubbed his fingers across his mouth, thinking of her deprived childhood. She had said that Debbie reminded her of herself. In what way? His sister led a charmed life—baby of the family, spoiled rotten with material goods, all the love in the universe. "Tell me about yourself."

She darted him a quick glance, then looked away, but not before he caught the shadowing of her blue eyes.

"Where did you go to college?" he asked, not content to let her retreat into a shell of reserve.

"At the University of Houston. Evening classes."

He wanted to know everything about her. She hadn't had an easy life. "Did you have a tough time getting your education, then getting started in the banking profession?"

She closed the drawer and turned halfway to face him. "It wasn't anything I couldn't handle."

"You're pretty self-sufficient, aren't you?"

"I've had to be. I've done what had to be done. I never sat around moping—I didn't have time for that. And I wouldn't have wanted to." She straightened to her full height. "Brent, the other day you accused me of butting into your affairs. I'll admit, I shouldn't have spoken to Jerry, but I wanted to help you any way I could. And if that meant giving my professional opinion, well... I'm proud of where I've gotten, and... my career is all I've ever had that lasted."

He tossed his glasses on the desk and levered away from his chair, striding to her side. Obviously trying not to look at him, she ducked away and hurried over to her desk to throw a cover over the typewriter. *Damn!* He had been making headway with her—best find neutral ground.

He slapped his palm against his thigh. "Say! I just had a brainstorm. Since you won't accept a salary from RSK, the least I can do is treat you to dinner."

"Thanks, but no thanks."

"I insist. Boss's orders."

She hesitated for what seemed to him like hours. Then wrinkling her nose, she shook her head. Smiling, she tapped a forefinger against her temple. "I've got a better idea. There's a seafood casserole in my freezer with your name all over it. I could fix up a salad and—"

Whoa! He wanted her on his own ground. "I won't hear of it. What kind of treat would that be for you? It's going to be a big, thick steak and a bottle of wine at the best restaurant in Corpus. Then, hmm, perhaps a bite of dessert at my place. And I won't take no for an answer."

Hands on her hips, she asked, "Are you trying to bully me?"

He grabbed his suit jacket, one finger hooking it over his shoulder. "Yep."

"Well, let's get one thing straight, Mr. Coulter. I'll agree to dinner." She smiled that fetching smile of hers. "But no dessert!"

Looping his arm through the crook of her elbow, he grinned mischievously. We'll see about that, he wanted to say, but he was learning patience where Cella was concerned.

"Cella, your wish is my command."

Sitting across from Brent in the softly lit restaurant, Marcella felt better than she had in days. The mellow tune of a violin wove sweet strains through the hushed voices of diners and the gentle tinkle of glasses and silverware. Nearby a tuxedoed waiter prepared Steak Diane; its luscious aroma filled the air, and its flames cast golden shadows. But more than anything, being with Brent was a pleasure.

And at that point the attraction she felt for Brent wasn't to be denied. Jim was a past mistake, which she couldn't completely disregard no matter what she felt for Brent. But right now she wanted nothing more than to forget yesterdays and to look forward to the future.

For tonight she would simply enjoy being with Brent.

When they had arrived he'd proven once again to be a take-charge person. He demanded a secluded table; he chose the Pinot noir—an excellent choice; he ordered dinner. The waiter snapped to attention at his courteous commands. Marcella didn't resent Brent's autocratic actions. Throughout her life she'd had to make all of her own decisions. It was marvelous to be pampered.

Yet she couldn't fully relax. Unanswered questions about Brent kept nagging at her. She was curious about what drove him to succeed, was more than curious about his feelings for his former wife. At the office she had wanted to quiz him, but he'd directed the conversation to her. Now she would find out!

"Brent, may I ask you a question?"

"Shoot."

"What does RSK stand for?"

"It's shorthand for risk." He eyed each of her features in turn. "That's the name of the wildcatter's game, Cella. Financial risk to discover petroleum. But I'm not telling you anything you wouldn't know, am I, banker lady?" he asked in a teasing voice.

"No." What was it about his smile that made her melt? "You're not scared of anything are you?"

"Nope." Brent swallowed hard. He had lied. He was damn scared of her and what she did to him.

"What made you decide to become a wildcatter?"

"My dad's been in and out of the business for years. I needed money for college, so it was natural for me to work in the oil fields during summer vacations. That first day on a rig I knew this was the life for me."

"It has a tendency to affect some men that way."

"I suppose. Anyway, after I graduated I worked as a petroleum engineer for an outfit out of Odessa. To finance RSK I put a few deals together on the side. Inherited a little money to put with it, too. And here I am."

"I wish you luck," she stated truthfully.

Brent studied her for a moment. She had sounded sincere. Of course, she sounded sincere about everything she said. He liked that in her. He also liked her thick black hair, but he wished it wasn't caught up in an old maid's bun. Those locks were too gorgeous not to be flowing down her back. Though tiny, she had an enormous capacity to fill a prim white blouse and make it sexier than hell. Her figure was awesome in that pencil-straight, navy blue skirt she wore. He'd been gawking at her all week, every time her back was turned at the office. It was great to have the opportunity to openly stare at her.

Reaching across the table, he covered her hand, squeezing lightly. "Something wrong with your dinner, honey?"

"I guess I'm not very hungry." She was filled with his presence; food wasn't on her mind. He was smiling his wonderful smile at her.

Candlelight flickered from a fluted holder and cast his lean features in glorious relief. She felt his knee brush, then stay by hers. Her heart missed a beat. His touch, in manner slight, was warm and daring and evocative of other touches...past moments.

Brent glanced at Cella's serene smile. He wanted to make her happy, and he realized that he had made a lot of mistakes with her. She had a deep reservoir of love and affection to be tapped. He wanted those feelings to wash over him, wanted to drown in those emotions. To lead her on about the future of their relationship would be a selfish move on his part, but...he was becoming a very greedy man when it came to her. He wanted to be number one in her life. At least for now.

Pushing his musings aside, he reached across the small table and sliced a tiny bite from her steak. As he waved the steak-laden fork slowly under her nose with his left hand, his right forefinger grazed the line of her jaw. "Tell me you missed me," he murmured huskily, compulsively.

Even a whisper of an admission would give him an edge fraught with danger to Marcella's psyche.

"Don't be—" The morsel slipped past her lips, and she chewed and swallowed the word *preposterous.* "Excuse me, but I thought this was a business dinner."

"Business dinner?" Giving her a puzzled look, he placed his fork atop his plate. "You're still upset about last Saturday night. Can you forgive me? I've forgiven you."

"Forgiven me?" she cried indignantly. She picked up her wineglass and sloshed deep red liquid on the tablecloth. Dabbing her napkin over the stain, she shook her head. "Brent Coulter, I have a hard time understanding you."

"Cella, I'm just a man." His hand covered hers. She went suddenly still. "A man who can think of nothing but you. I watch you at work," he admitted in a raspy whisper, blatant with sexual need. "And then I go home, and I can't sleep. I lie in bed and fantasize about what it would be like to have you. Sweet mercies, there's only a thin wall separating us at night. I want to take an ax to that barrier, then make you mine." He lifted her palm, kissing the center. "I want this hand to touch me, and I want to touch and taste and satisfy every inch of your naked body." His eyes were burning into her. "Is that so difficult to understand?"

She was weak. Wanting and needing him with the same fierceness that he had expressed, she ached to give in to the liquid heaviness that settled in the center of her femininity. It would be so easy to lean across the table, to bury the pad of her finger in the deep cleft of his chin and to admit that she ached to learn the secrets of his lovemaking. But she shouldn't—wouldn't! Sex without mutual love was unthinkable.

"You have a one-track mind," she replied teasingly.

"Guilty." His eyelids were heavy with longing. "I'm a man possessed—and starving for . . . dessert."

She had to pull in the reigns of her emotions. There was only one course of action: invite his ire. She could handle his anger better than she could deal with her own weaknesses. And this was the lead-in to the solution to his monetary problems.

Her voice took on its most businesslike tone. "Debbie mentioned that Jerry Hagen wants to invest in RSK."

She steeled herself for the verbal blow.

But Brent wasn't angry. For some odd reason he trusted Cella. But he did regret that she hadn't responded to his heartfelt invitation. Taking a deep breath, he willed his aroused body to return to normal. He was pushing her too fast again. Her hesitancy was understandable. He hadn't exactly been a knight in shining armor—but he'd change that. She needed to learn to trust him. All right. If she wanted to talk business, he was game. He had all the time in the world, and he had to make this moment count.

"You heard right. Hagen wants to buy a partnership."

"Please don't think I'm trying to meddle, but is he financially able to swing the deal?"

"He has a friend in Houston who's willing to back him in a joint venture."

"How do you feel about that?"

"Lousy." He reached into his jacket pocket for a cigarette, then offered her one. She declined with a shake of her head. He inhaled the smoke while dousing the match's flame with a quick shake of his hand. Leaning back in his chair, he studied the wall behind her. "I'm not going for it. RSK is *my* company."

"Brent, without private financing, how can you continue to operate? You'll be the first to admit there's a great deal more drilling to be done. Drilling contractors don't come cheap. Plus you have salaries and overhead at the office to consider—"

Cutlery and china jumped when he pounded the table. "Marcella, I'm not an idiot. You don't have to remind me of my responsibilities."

"Why don't you talk with Mr. Goodman about a loan?"

"Out of the question." Brent downed his glass of wine, ordering himself to settle down—for her sake. His company, especially as it related to Sneed Goodman, was a bone of contention with him, but he refused to make another mistake with Cella.

"Why?" she asked quickly.

"I'd rather not go into that."

"If you won't give up sole ownership, you have to give the alternatives consideration. Goodman National has an obligation to you, Brent." She had ceased wanting to make him angry; she genuinely wanted to help him. She lightened her tone. "You're a depositor in the bank. We're in business to make money from loans. At least give us the chance."

"I can pull RSK out of this temporary bind without your help, thank you very much," Brent replied, thinking about his last-ditch plan. He hadn't told anyone about it and didn't want to. If known, it might tear his family apart.

"How?" she asked boldly. "Be practical, for heaven's sake. If you won't talk with Mr. Goodman and if Jerry can arrange private financing, let him do it."

"How in the world did I ever manage to get by for thirty years without your advice?" he asked, irony tinting his words. "Dammit, Marcella, I may not be perfect, but why do you have a total lack of faith in me and in my abilities?"

"Brent Coulter, don't accuse me of not having faith in you, because I do! What I'm trying to get across is that if you have a chance to solve your cash flow problems, go for it. It's good business. Faith has nothing to do with it."

Brent motioned for the check. She was right. Damn her and her logical mind. Why in hell's name couldn't he have fallen for some vacuous little airhead? Cella was as smart as Vicky. No! She's smarter than Ms. Goodman-Coulter, he surmised irritably, yet proudly. And Cella's a helluva lot prettier, too. The woman was an enigma. She was as aggressive as a tiger, profession-wise. But when she wanted to be, she was as gentle as a kitten. Cella was going to be the death of him, he bemoaned inwardly while throwing some bills on the table.

He captured her arm and escorted her to his convertible. A thousand stars illuminated her face, yet failed to capture the breathlessness of her beauty, he thought with a blithe glow in his heart.

Once in the car, he leaned across the seat and captured her lips in a heated kiss. "I'm hungry for something sweet. How about you?" he asked thickly, dragging his mouth from hers.

Marcella was still reeling from his kiss. She had to be strong! She hadn't made him angry in the restaurant. But he had another weak point....

"No, thank you. Didn't you know an excessive amount of 'sweets' can be harmful to your health? Your body chemistry gets all out of whack and before you know it, you're saying and doing things you wouldn't normally dream possible."

"I certainly hope so."

"Then let me warn you, Mr. Coulter. Habits are hard to break with me. Once I acquired a sweet tooth I'd get fat and sassy."

"A little extra weight wouldn't hurt you."

"You might not be able to shake off my extra poundage."

Turning his face toward the dashboard's green lumination, he rubbed his eyes. "In other words you're telling me it's all or nothing with you. Right?"

She nodded slowly.

"I was afraid of that," he muttered.

Her ploy to make him think twice before trifling with her heart had worked, she realized with a twinge of regret as he fired the engine. But she wasn't going to settle for less than his body, mind and soul. Would he ever have that much to give?

They began the short drive back to Port Merritt. A soft tune emanated from the car radio, and the wind brushed her face and hair. Marcella didn't speak and neither did Brent. She was weary, weary from an exhausting week at work, but especially depleted from fighting her star-crossed attraction to Brent. The temptation to close her eyes, for only a moment, overcame her.

Her tension abated. She felt weightless, as if floating. Then in her dream a tall, flaxen-haired man folded her into his muscular arms. There were no cares, no problems, only love and tender protection.... Her hands explored, caressed and molded warm, hard muscles. A big hand cupped her derriere, pulling her closer.

Deep timbred and smooth, his voice whispered. "We're home, Sleeping Beauty."

"Nooo," she murmured drowsily, more than half-asleep, "jus' wanna cuddle you." She snuggled closer against the sheltering warmth. Tenderly a mouth touched hers...Brent's lips. Brent! Oh, Lord—she hadn't been dreaming! Mortified by her actions, she pulled back violently.

"Woman, you're a wildcat." His mouth was twitching. "There may be hope for us yet."

She buried her face in her hands. "I—I can't believe I did that."

"You won't hear any complaints from me." He slid across the seat, easing her face against his chest. "Hey, don't be embarrassed." Grazing the wisps of hair around her temple, he touched a kiss to the top of her head. "I took the pins out of your hair when you were sleeping. Mind?"

"No," she admitted as he finger-combed her hair.

"Cella, I haven't felt this good in a long time. Matter of fact, I've been thinking about what you said when we left the restaurant. I'm thinking a sugar addiction might not be such a bad thing to have."

"Are you sure?"

"Let's explore the possibilities." His hands urged her to meet his gaze, and he looked deeply into her eyes. "We agreed, not long after we met, to get to know each other better. It's been rocky since then. I'd still like to get to know you better."

"I feel the same about you, Brent."

"Good. And in the meantime I don't want to push you. But rest assured, when you're ready—I'll be ready."

A wave of exuberance swept through her. Brent would do things on her terms! Fully awake now, she realized the car was parked in front of their duplex.

"Brent, the light's are on in your house," she stated, puzzled.

"It's some of my buddies." He looked a bit sheepish. "We play poker once a month, and I forgot it was my night to play host." He went on to explain that one of the men had a key to his house. "Can I interest you in a game of chance?"

"Why not?" she returned, laughing softly. "I love to play games."

No doubt in Brent's mind, she was a master of games. Of the heart, anyway. Truth be known, he was a gambling man. And Cella Parker was a chance worth taking.

Three men were gathered around Brent's breakfast table. A haze of smoke as thick as fog haloed the card players. Brent proudly introduced her.

A roughneck who worked for the Rollins One's drilling contractor, Allen Zimmerman, was wiry, brown-haired and well into his beers. She'd seen him before; he'd been one of the karate enthusiasts at Brent's house that first night. He sized her up with a wolf-on-the-prowl look, and she immediately decided she didn't like him.

Amigo Drilling's tool pusher, Frank Hocker, seemed rather quiet. Gary Cooper personified—yes, ma'am; no, ma'am; nice to meet ya, ma'am. She found it easy to like the rig boss.

The last fellow, Woody Athersby, a courtly gentleman of about fifty-five, nursed a cordial glass of crème de menthe. She learned that he held the office of county sheriff and was himself an investor in another oil rig. His kind hazel eyes and his gentle smile reminded Marcella of her father.

Brent, his wallet out, pulled several large bills from the pocket. "I'll stake you, Cella."

"No," she answered shortly, shaken out of her remembrance of days gone by. "I'll play with my own money."

Brent pulled up a chair, placing her between him and Woody at the crowded round table, and she felt Brent's thigh firmly against hers. These men reminded her of the oil field hands who had gathered around her father's kitchen table, so many years before. Rounds of cards were punctuated with oil field talk and jokes as the men added cans and ashes to the room's clutter. But Marcella wasn't disturbed by the bachelor quarter's mess—memories of her father were crashing through her thoughts.

The deal passed to Frank. "Draw. Five-dollar ante." He counted out five cards to each player.

"Hey, Coulter," Allen Zimmerman drawled, a cigarette hanging from the corner of his mouth as he gave Marcella the once-over. "You sure gotta pretty lady."

"Yeah. Play your cards, Zimmerman," Brent said tersely.

"Say, beautiful, when you get sicka ol' Coulter, gimme a call."

Brent leaned forward. "Another crack like that, Zimmerman, and you'll be eating your teeth."

"Don't get all hot and bothered, buddy. I was joking." Allen shot a look around the table. "Sure don't want ol' black belt Coulter to karate chop me."

"Yeah, well, keep that in mind," Brent said, picking up his cards and easing back his chair.

When Woody laughed at Brent's obvious jealousy, Marcella tensed. The sweet ring to his tenor resounded through her. So much, so much like Curtis Parker he had sounded.

"It's your bet, ma'am," Frank reminded.

"I heard you." Control yourself, Marcella, she cautioned. If she didn't she would lose the tenuous grip on her composure. She tried to concentrate on the game.

"Cella, are you okay?" Brent inquired tenderly.

"Everything's just marvelous," she replied tersely. She upped the ante another five dollars and took one card. Brent traded three cards; Allen Zimmerman, a sly smirk on his face, traded one; and the dealer folded. Woody took two.

She wanted desperately to leave. "Call," she announced in a mutter.

When it was his turn Allen Zimmerman pompously showed his hand. "Full house." He winked at Marcella. "Can ya beat that, little lady?"

After Woody Athersby folded she answered laconically. "You're beat, Mr. Zimmerman. Royal flush."

Brent studied her. She was acting strange. Aloof. Did she resent the guys for being there simply because a cozy evening had been interrupted? He wanted nothing more than to be alone with her. But who was he trying to kid? She would have given him a good-night kiss at her front door. Period.

He concluded that it was nothing more than her transferring her dislike of oil rigs to his friends because they worked one. And he didn't like that. As play continued for the next hour, her attitude didn't change.

"Folks," Woody announced, standing up, "stakes're too high for me. I'm calling it quits. It was a pleasure to meet you, Marcella," he finished, extending his hand.

Marcella's hand shook. If she touched this man who reminded her so much of her father, she would fall to pieces.

Woody withdrew his arm and said his farewells.

Brent was fuming. Who did she think she was, treating his friends as if they were dirt under her feet? Especially Woody—a greater guy had never walked the earth!

He leaned over to whisper, "I don't know what's the matter with you, but you could try acting a little nicer. If I'm remembering correctly, you've had a lot of experience dealing with poker-playing oil-patch rowdies."

Immediately he realized the folly of his words. Damn!

Hurt and anger startled Marcella out of her former shock. He was taunting her with a confidence, spoken from the depths of her soul, that day at the rig. His cruel, thoughtless words ate through her like acid. Vicious streams of betrayal lanced through her. Jim Turley had known bits and pieces of her childhood, had realized the pain it caused. And he'd used that information to his best advantage when they had quarreled.

"Why don't I get you gentlemen another round of beers?" she asked with saccharin sweetness, grabbing for an excuse to get away.

Brent tried to catch her hand. She hastened from his presence.

Marcella needed fresh air. The beach. The beautiful, peaceful sounds and smells of the Gulf would help her. Noiselessly she closed the door behind her.

Pulling off her shoes in the grass flats, she headed for the solace of the surf. She would walk and walk until Brent Coulter was completely out of her mind. In the darkness she silently trod, trying to let herself drift with the sea breezes.

"Marcella!" she heard Brent roar.

## Chapter Six

Go away!" Marcella yelled, tugging her skirt above her knees to run as fast as she could from the sound of Brent's approaching footsteps. The ocean's roar was as deafening as the racing of her blood.

"Cella, wait!"

Suddenly her toe thwacked against a chunk of driftwood—pain knifed up her leg as she stumbled. Instantly the iron grip of his arms clamped her, jerking backward.

"Let me go," she ordered furiously, struggling against the tight bonds. Dwarfed by his sheer size, she felt tears of helplessness fill her eyes as his arm swung under her knees and he crushed her to his chest. "Put me down!"

Fluidly he dropped to the sand, Marcella in his

arms. To her distress, she was sitting on his lap, but somehow she didn't have the strength to move.

"I hurt your feelings, Cella, and I'm sorry." His fingers spread as they combed through the hair at her nape. With gentle pressure he pressed her cheek against his shoulder. "The minute you left it dawned on me something was wrong with you. Please tell me."

"Don't ever—ever!—bring up anything related to my childhood."

"Oh, baby, I'm a heel, and I'd give anything to take back what I said. Believe me, I didn't mean to hurt you," he said gently. "When you acted like you were better than the guys, I got hot under the collar."

"'Better than the guys'?" she repeated in confusion. "That never entered my mind."

Pulling back, she gazed deeply into his eyes. All at once the fight went out of her. She had been vulnerable and let her emotions run away with her at the poker game. In slow, deliberate words she told him of Woody's uncanny resemblance to her father, then confessed the pain—omitting the part about living with him—that Jim Turley had inflicted upon her when he'd cut her out of his life.

"He never shared anything of himself with me," she finished. "I wanted to know about his fears, his hopes. But he wasn't open about himself."

Brent tilted her chin with the crook of his finger, forcing her to look at him. His eyes were warm, reflecting his concerns. "He hurt you bad...."

"Yes," she admitted in a ragged whisper. Then in an effort to put aside those remembrances she said lightly, "I was being loony, I guess. Didn't I warn you not to tangle with me when the moon's full?"

He chuckled. "And what did I say about a lover's moon, baby?" he whispered, reminding her of that first evening at the beach. "The ol' man up there's not full anymore, but let's pretend he is."

"What am I going to do with you?" she asked with mock exasperation, sliding her arm around his shoulder. "Wait! Don't answer that."

"Why not?" he teased. One hand began to move in tiny circles up her back, his other smoothly unfastening a button of her blouse. Feeling his arousal against her hip, she trembled. Roughened fingertips slipping beneath the lace edge of her bra, he caressed her tenderly. "Want to know the real reason I got miffed tonight?"

"Y-yes," she answered, dizzy from his ardent touches.

"I wanted to be alone with you," he confessed, the low ring of his baritone spreading as richly as honey through her veins.

"Why... didn't you... tell them to leave?"

His head dipped to her throat, and he trailed kisses of fire to the lobe of her ear. "Would you've let me be alone with you?"

"Pr-probably not."

She was burning, singed by his touch. And if she didn't pull away from the fevered claim of his artful embrace only smoke and ashes from her shattered defenses would be left in morning's light. She longed to give in, to be consumed by the flame of shared passion... but she couldn't. She needed the assurance of unwavering love. She wiggled onto the sand, sitting next to him, and stared unseeingly at the arrowhead-shaped lights of an offshore rig painting the watery horizon.

For a long moment he didn't speak. Then, a slight frown bracketing his mouth, he turned to her and swept the long fall of black hair away from her cheek.

"Cella, I want to be open with you." He stretched his legs out, bracing himself with his elbows on the sand behind him. "Want to hear my troubles?"

Drawing her knees up, she hugged them to her chest. "I'd like that very much."

His voice was barely above a whisper. "Risks...and failure." He picked up a handful of sand, letting it run slowly through his fingers. "They scare the bejesus out of me."

"Oh, Brent," she said, reaching over to squeeze his hand. "No one's immune to the fear of failure. It's a very human feeling."

"Yeah, but I have to succeed with RSK."

"You strike me as a man who'd land on his feet, no matter what the situation." She remembered him in his office making snap decisions, never doubting his beliefs. "But why is success so important to you?"

"Because my father's a failure. Damn, I could use a cigarette." He ran his hand along his scalp. "The old man can sniff out petroleum like you wouldn't believe. But he's a joke in the oil patch. He can't keep a dollar. This may sound crazy to you, but I want to bring respect in the industry back to the Coulter name." He laughed, throwing his head back. "Aw, hell, I wanna be rich, too."

"But—"

"Cella, at this point in my life, RSK's success means more to me than anything in the world. Well, uh—" he grinned teasingly "—that's not quite true."

She caught his innuendo. Nudging his shoulder, she prodded, "Go on with what you were talking about—before!"

"All right, for Pete's sake. About Goodman National extending me a loan: when I was laying the groundwork for RSK, Sneed warned me not to get into the business." He chuckled halfheartedly. "It goes without saying, I didn't take his advice. I wanted to make it on my own. But, cripes, you're the officer on my accounts, you work in my office, you know my financial situation. RSK has to strike it big, or I'm back to square one. And I can't let that happen."

This sharing of his innermost thoughts reached into the depth of Marcella's soul. This proud man never seemed more human.

"And I wonder about you, Cella," he continued. "I wonder if I'm doing the right thing with you."

"What do you mean?"

"I don't want to hurt you." He leaned to his side; his fingers curled around her wrist, then moved up her forearm. "That jerk broke your heart, and I don't want to do the same thing. But you see I've got my own demons to fight. And they stop me from getting in over my head with you. I'd like to make a clean sweep of the past and start over...but it's not that easy."

Cautiously, Marcella asked, "Brent, do you still care for your ex-wife?"

He levered to his feet and extended a hand to her. "Come on. Let's take a walk."

He finally spoke when they were strolling along the sand, arm in arm. "Vicky's a good person. I'd trust her with my life."

"Brent, what happened?"

"Lack of interest." He kicked at a piece of debris. "Vicky's a gung-ho career woman, and when we got married I didn't have a problem with that. Everyone's entitled to do what they want in life, but her job came between us. She wanted to be married, but she didn't want to make any of the sacrifices. Call me selfish—I wanted to share a life with her. She didn't see it that way. Her number-one priority was always the boardroom rather than us." His fingers grazed her cheek. "If you were in love you wouldn't be guilty of that, would you, Cella?"

Marcella pondered his words. She had devoted her life to her career. Would she be able to give it up— lock, stock and barrel?

"At one time I was willing to give up everything I've worked hard to attain. To be honest, I considered it when I was with Jim. I gave him everything I had to give emotionally, and it got me nothing." She looked him squarely in the eye. "I'd have to be very sure of a special man's everlasting love before I'd consider giving up my career."

Her words gave Brent food for thought. He needed time to think. "Cella, it's getting late...."

"Why don't we start back?" she asked as if she sensed his inner turmoil.

He had plenty of time to think while wearing a trail in his carpet that night, grasping for answers. Cella meant the world to him. In fact he thought he might be falling in love with her. What was the answer?

Marry Cella? No way. Live with her? Maybe. But would he be falling back into that old trap of expecting too much, receiving too little?

What he needed was time—time to decide what to do about Cella Parker. And with time, maybe the answers would work out for themselves. He could corral a few guys and go fishing. No. That was out. He'd camp out at the rig in the meantime; he could stay busy there. If he stayed around the house, he was certain to run into Cella. He wouldn't risk it.

As the hours turned into one day, then four, Marcella was edgy about the tomblike silence from Brent's duplex, from Brent himself. A strange emptiness hollowed within her. Had he given up on her? Please don't let that be true, she prayed.

Earlier that evening she'd decided to eat away her problems. Hang the weekly food budget; Veal Sylvie was roasting in the oven. Spinach braised in cream sauce and herbed tomatoes were set for final preparations. But the idea of a solo feast did little to ease her loneliness.

She spooned out a special treat for Mona Lisa, who twined her body around and around Marcella's legs and meowed in her scratchy Siamese style.

Marcella bent down, bowl in hand. Running her palm along the cat's sleek coat as the feline gobbled down the mackerel, Marcella spoke.

"Brent never answered my question. What do you think, Mona Lisa? Does he still love Vicky?" The cat ignored her. "Selfish," she chided, then laughed. "Wow, I've really hit the bottom, pouring out my troubles to a cat."

Suddenly Marcella heard sounds of life from Brent's side of the duplex. He was home! Would he come over? Should she go over there? What would she say?

She glanced at her wristwatch. Seven o'clock. "I'll give him exactly one hour, then I'm going to take matters into my own hands."

At precisely 8:00 p.m. she was standing at his front door, ringing the bell. The door flew open. At a loss for words, she felt her mouth become dry. My, she had forgotten how truly handsome he was! He smiled. She colored slightly and laced her fingers.

"Hi, Cella," he greeted with a slight growl.

"Welcome home. Could you—I was wondering— Um." *Be brave!* "Brent, the light's burned out in my bedroom, and I can't get the fixture loose. Will you please help me?"

Grinning, he gave a mock salute. "Brent Coulter, white knight, at your service, ma'am."

Brent looped arms with Cella, escorting her next door. The past few days, fighting for sanity, Brent had been miserable. He'd finally decided to come home when he realized he couldn't avoid her forever.

If he had any sense, though, he would call an electrician to help her and leave immediately. He cast a sidelong glance at Cella. Gorgeous. Her long black hair swished down her back. The baby blue of her V-necked jersey blouse intensified her sky-blue eyes, not to mention her ample cleavage. Her white shorts emphasized the shapeliness of her legs, legs that were incredibly long for her height.

The enticing scent of simmering food permeated her house, which was neat as a pin and reeked of homey ambience. Much like his parents' home. He admired that quality in Cella. No, an electrician wouldn't be necessary, he decided as he followed her to her room.

Looking sideways at her antique four-poster bed, he cleared his throat. Being in Cella's bedroom did wild things to his libido. He was of a good mind to sweep her into his arms and find out what it would be like with her on that lacy, eyelet bedspread. *Settle down, old boy.*

He stepped onto the wobbly stepladder positioned under the light. "Whoa! I'm too heavy for this thing. Better hold on to my legs, Cella."

Falling flat on his face would be better than the consequences of having her so near, yet so far away. The delicate scent of her perfume wafted to his nostrils. With her arms wrapped around his legs and with her generous breasts crushed against the side of his thigh, he was dying. Dying. His hands shook as he loosened the fixture.

"Give me that light bulb," he ordered brokenly, casting a look at her. She placed the bulb in his hand. Who could blame him for holding her fingers a moment too long?

"Do you need anything else?" she asked in her sweet, dulcet voice.

"Don't tempt me, woman."

Marcella was transfixed as she watched him finish the chore. Laying her cheek against his hip, she never wanted to release him. There was a slight woodsy scent to Brent, mixed with the warmth of his male body. Her attention was riveted to the male bulge that stretched his khaki trousers. Wantonly, she didn't look away.

"I'm finished," he stated. "You can let go now."

"Oh." She stepped back. "Well, uh, thanks for taking care of the light."

"No problem." Dusting his hands, he jumped to the floor and strode out of the room. "Guess I'd better be running along."

"Wait! Brent, have you had dinner?"

"No," he admitted.

"Wonderful!" She smiled with all the coquettish charm she could muster. "Will you share dinner with me? It's so lonesome eating alone."

"Uh, well..."

In minutes he was seated across from her in the dining room. The table was set with her best china and crystal, but no candles. That would have been too obvious, she had reasoned.

Mona Lisa jumped to his lap.

"She's an extremely ill-mannered pest at times. She's picked up the terrible habit of panhandling lately," Marcella explained, watching the cat rub her jaw against his chest. "She's really taken with you. Funny, she never likes people."

"She loves me. Guess I have a way with women," he teased.

"That you do," she replied. Truer words were never spoken.

"I've been feeding her," he admitted.

"What!"

"She comes over and eats out of Fred's dish. They nap together, too."

Astonished, she said, "But I've been careful to keep her in. How did she get in to your house?"

"I checked it out. There's a small hole, just big enough for her to slide through, between our laundry cabinets." He winked, then leaned to touch Marcella's cheek. "If I made the hole bigger, what would it take to entice you over to nap with me?"

She was saved from answering when Mona Lisa clawed his leg and he yelped as the cat jumped from his lap.

"Way with women, huh?" Marcella asked, handing Brent the wine bottle.

"Shut your mouth, woman, and let's eat."

After serving a man-size portion of the ham-and-cheese-stuffed veal roast, she smiled sweetly and handed him the plate. "I hope you like veal."

"Love it," he fibbed. He wasn't about to hurt her feelings by telling her that he was strictly a steak-and-potatoes man. Besides, he was enjoying this softer, more old-fashioned side of her.

Yet her domesticity frightened him, brought to mind the institution of marriage. Or at least what he reckoned marriage ought to be. He had never told her, but he steered clear of her offers of a home-cooked meal for that reason.

Gingerly he tasted his food. "Hey, this is good!" he stated truthfully.

"I'm glad you like it."

If he stayed in this atmosphere, Brent realized, Cella would get further under his skin than she already was. He could grow very used to this.

He replaced his knife and fork, then wiped his mouth with a linen napkin. "We need to talk."

Marcella eyed him hesitantly. "All right."

"We've been playing cat and mouse. I think it's time we cleared the air."

"Your're right," she replied, dread filling her.

"Cella, I want you in my life, but I don't want to mislead you. I want to make love to you—not once, but over and over and over. But if and when we do make love, I want you to realize up-front that there'll be no strings attached."

"Strings?" Marcella asked.

"Marriage."

"I don't remember proposing, Brent."

Red crept past his collar and up to his face. "But aren't you holding out for—"

"I'm not a beggar. I'm not holding my hand out for anything. But you can make book on this—I don't go in for simple flings."

Brent opened his mouth to say something, then closed it. He rose and picked up his plate, taking it to the kitchen. "I'll help you with these dishes. Then I'd better be going."

"Leave the dishes."

"I guess it's good-night. . . ."

"Yes."

After Brent had gone Marcella raked their unfinished dinner into the disposal and brooded over his words. "No strings attached." She needed those strings. Her feelings for him were too special, too precious to risk on a casual affair. It wouldn't have been fair to either of them if she gave into their physical desire and ended up asking more from him than he was willing to give. Especially since he had made his intentions positively clear.

Once in her lonely bed she stared at the wall separating her from Brent. Marcella wished with every beat of her heart that the ghosts of haunted yesterdays did not shadow the promise of all their tomorrows.

If only it weren't that way, how marvelous their relationship could have been. But she had to face reality. Life is full of if-onlys. She wouldn't hand her heart to a man who couldn't love and be loved. Experience had taught her that.

Time went by slowly for Marcella. The days were easier to handle than the nights. The evenings stretched interminably long as she searched for chores to keep her busy. And when she retired to her empty bed she tossed and turned, thinking of Brent.

At least the days were filled with mountains of time-occupying work. That was solace to a certain degree. But her responsibilities at the bank were taxing. By Friday afternoon at closing time, she was mentally exhausted. She leaned back in her leather office chair, rubbing her temples. The day had been grueling. State banking examiners had shown up the previous morning to conduct an unexpected audit, a practice always expected in banking, but never welcomed. On top of the Gang of Three auditors, Bernice Prothro had seemed to take a certain pleasure in pestering Marcella about nitpicky details of a loan she had extended to the financially pressed owner of a dump truck company.

But Marcella wasn't looking forward to the weekend. Impulsively she decided to call up a few old friends in Houston and try to drum up a weekend trip away from Port Merritt...and thoughts of Brent Coulter.

Easing her chair to face the window, she picked up the telephone receiver. Her fingertip on a button, she jumped at a familiar male voice.

"So this is how the lady banker spends her days, lollygagging at her desk."

She swung around, the coasters of her chair creaking. Brent was lazing in the office doorway, one hand on the jamb, one foot crossed over the other.

"Good afternoon," she said politely. "And to what do I owe this honor?"

"T.G.I.F." Pushing away from the doorframe, he strode toward her. "I thought you might be interested in a happy-hour drink."

Aligning her pen with her pencil, she forced her vision to her desk pad. "Sorry. I have other plans."

"Break them."

Anger swept through her. "Why don't you leave me alone?"

"I can't."

"You can."

"I won't." He dropped into the chair opposite her. "And you will," he stated confidently.

"Why should I?"

"What did I tell you about questioning destiny?" he asked smoothly.

"Are we destined for each other, Brent?"

"I don't want to give up on what we have, Cella. Do you?"

Marcella was reluctant to follow the logic of her heart. If she left the bank with Brent, well, her equanimity couldn't withstand another confrontation, another letdown. She looked at him, looked beneath the handsome surface to the person who lived within him. Brent was a good man, kind and considerate. He hadn't lied to her about what he wanted and didn't want. Wouldn't it be wrong to deny themselves a chance to explore the possibility that what they shared might be more than a fleeting attraction?

"No. I don't want to give up. I'd love to have a drink with you."

"That's my girl!" He surged to his feet, extending his hand to her. "Come along, Cella love, my chariot awaits."

Had he meant to call her love? she wondered. She hoped so. She grabbed her briefcase, which he took from her hand, and they started for...their destiny.

"Ms. Parker," Bernice croaked, halting Marcella's footsteps. "You're not leaving early, are you? Where's your girl? She borrowed my DDA file, and I want it back—now!"

Marcella, boiling at Bernice's high-handed impertinence, eyed the head bookkeeper, whose lip was curled. She was not leaving early, but had no desire to get into a petty argument with a subordinate.

"Mrs. Prothro, I do not have a 'girl.' I have a very competent secretary by the name of Ms. Bates. Furthermore, Ms. Bates left a message on your desk indicating the bank examiners needed to audit your DDA file."

"Hello there, Bernie," Brent interrupted.

"Mrs. Prothro to you," the woman said acidly.

"Well, Mrs. Prothro, you old crone, I'm surprised to see you're still at the bank." He patted her cheek. "When are you going to retire and give Goodman National a break?"

Bernice's gray eyes narrowed. "I can see you're still as arrogant and impertinent as ever, Brent Coulter."

"Aw, Bernie." Brent laughed. "You never could take a joke."

Turning on the ball of her foot, Bernice flipped a thin shoulder, muttering under her breath, "I'll speak with you Monday, Ms. Parker."

"Now you have something to look forward to," he whispered in Marcella's ear as they again headed for the front door.

"Don't be too rough on her, Brent. She's—" Marcella paused, trying to think of a good quality that Mrs. Prothro possessed "—she's dedicated to Goodman National."

"She's dedicated to making everyone's life miserable." He squeezed her hand. "Let's change the subject."

And change the subject they did. Within minutes Marcella was sitting next to Brent in a wooden booth of the local tavern. The room was crowded with people who were all apparently intent on making the most of week's end. Neon lights and plastic signs advertised various brands of beer; country music blared from the juke box. An indiscernible sweetness that was not unpleasant filled the air, as well as hazy tendrils of cigarette smoke that curled toward the ceiling.

Brent's long frame aligned with the petiteness of Marcella's. She sipped a Scotch and soda; he drank a beer. The music changed to a slow melody.

"Care to dance?" he asked quietly.

Wordlessly he led her to the postage-stamp-size dance floor. He drew her hands to his shoulders.

"I want to hold you close, Cella."

She felt his palms cross at her waist. He moved with gentle grace, the grace of a man who had danced a thousand times. And each time marvelously. She buried her cheek against the rock wall of his chest. And with the gentle sway of his body she became more and more aware of Brent, the prospective lover. And the thought was exhilarating.

The song ended and another song began, a little faster in beat, yet still romantic. He trailed tiny kisses across her forehead. Burning with desire, she arched against him. She felt his hands slide to her derriere, cupping her to him.

"This is what you do to me, Cella baby."

"It's... You're positively indecent," she murmured, not at all offended by his unmistakable arousal.

"I'm not ashamed of what you do to me. Are you?"

"No," she replied, smiling demurely.

"Would I be pressing my luck if I asked you to leave with me?"

"Y-yes." But she wasn't convinced that she wouldn't welcome the moments alone with Brent. He danced her over to their booth and slid in after her.

His arm crossed her shoulder, and he blew a thin stream of air into her ear. She shivered with delight.

"Then I'll have to work on my luck," he murmured, his free hand caressing her thigh. "I want you to have a drink at my place. That is, if that's what you want, too."

Her body seemed as if it were boneless, and her heartbeat was pounding. With every breath in her body she wanted to make love with him. But she needed, demanded to know about his feelings for Vicky. It was imperative.

"Brent, do you still love Vicky?"

He pulled back. "Hell, no!"

"Are you sure?" she asked, needing reassurance.

He captured her face between his palms. His thumbs rubbed the sensitive area behind her earlobes.

"I love *you*, Marcella Parker." As Brent voiced those three little words he realized the quintessential truth of his admission. Their problems could be worked out, someway. He loved this woman with a passion that he'd never before experienced. "Why do you think I asked you out tonight? I've given a lot of thought to you and me as a couple. And, baby, nothing would please me more."

"Or me," she whispered in return, her heart singing. He loved her! And in her jubilation the shackles that bound her set her free.

"Do you love me, Cella?"

"Oh, yes—yes. Yes!"

"Then say it, Cella. Tell me."

"I love you, Brent Coulter."

And caught up in the breathlessness of the moment she placed her palm against his beloved cheek, running her fingers through the thick hair above his sideburn. Her prayers had been answered. And she was thankful for this second chance. This *better* chance with Brent. He would never let her down.

"Brent darling, you were saying something about a drink at your place...?"

## Chapter Seven

Marcella hesitated at Brent's door. She wanted the evening to go on forever and with no interruptions. But she had a responsibility to Mona Lisa.

"Brent," she said, "will you excuse me for a minute?"

Holding her elbows, he pulled her close. "I'm not going to hear that old saw about 'slipping into something comfortable,' am I? Believe me, baby, you're going to be comfortable enough."

"No, silly," she replied, giggling. "I need to feed Mona Lisa."

"Damn that cat. It's a sad night when a man plays second fiddle to a Siamese...."

She turned her face up to protest, and he slanted his mouth over hers, touching in minute degrees the tiny hollow that marked the curve of her upper lip. The brush of his mustache tickled her in the most pleasant of ways. Suddenly his demanding lips and tongue possessed her, and with her hands gripping his shoulders for support, she melted against him, returning the fire of his kiss. And all too soon he drew back, his eyes caressing her.

"I've been aching for you, sweetheart. Do you know how much I want to be inside you right now?"

His wickedly seductive question, needing no answer, raised tiny bumps on her arms. "B-but it'll only take a minute to feed her," she protested weakly.

"I'll go with you."

"What about poor Fredi? Don't you need to feed and walk her? If you don't attend to her now, *I'll* be usurped by your dog...."

He rested his chin on the top of her head, as if to cool his ardor. "Sometimes, woman, you're entirely too practical," he bemoaned gruffly. Swatting her backside, he ordered, "You've got exactly five minutes. If you're not in my house, I'll be over to get you."

Brent practically flew to his house. Wow! He felt great; this was a far cry from the loneliness he'd experienced over the past four days. Cella was a woman who knew what she wanted, and he was a man who wanted her. He loved her, really loved her. And the evening had just begun.

Throwing open his front door, he almost didn't see the white envelope that had been slipped under the doorway. He picked it up, turning it over in his hand. His name was written on the front in scratchy penmanship. He tore the envelope open, reading the letter once, and again.

Staring with unseeing eyes at the wall, he crumbled the paper in his fist.

Marcella sang one of the tunes they had danced to in the tavern as she fed her cat. She couldn't wait to get back to Brent! After freshening up she sailed over to his duplex.

But after she entered his bachelor quarters, with its modern decor, she realized something was awry. Brent's temperament was drastically changed; gone was his loving spirit of only a few minutes ago. His tanned face was pale. Frown lines grooved his forehead and bracketed his mouth. A sinking feeling dipped through her as she huddled on the sofa, watching him pace the floor.

"Did you take care of Fredi?" she asked, eyeing the Doberman who was staring at her master with soulful eyes.

"Yeah." He ran his fingers through his hair. "Let me get you a drink."

"Thank you," she replied, unable to read his strange mood.

She followed him to the kitchen. He threw ice cubes into two glasses and sloshed overgenerous amounts of Scotch in them. She perched on the countertop. After wordlessly handing her a tumbler, he downed the liquor in one swallow.

Her voice wavered as she asked, "Have I done something wrong?"

"Oh, baby, no!" He walked to her, pulling her head against his shoulder. "Not by a long shot."

Desperate to draw him out of the doldrums, she searched for something to say. "How's it going at the rig?"

"A-okay."

"Gosh, I had a really tough week at the bank," she confided, at a loss to think of anything better to impart. "We've had auditors in for the past two days, and it was murder."

"I could use another drink," he stated, moving away to refill his glass. "How about you?"

"No, thanks." She took a sip of whisky. Make him talk, she ordered herself. "Of course, we're not worried about the audit, Mr. Goodman said—"

"Don't mention that man's name to me," he roared.

Oh, Lord, what happened? she wondered. Had Sneed Goodman telephoned Brent or something? "Please talk to me, Brent."

Placing his glass down, he walked to face her. He grasped her wrists, then kissed her palms. "I love you, baby. But I—I can't talk about... I'm sorry, Cella love, but this is something I've got to work out for myself. Right now I need time to think."

Marcella sighed in frustration. Her attempts at small talk had been fruitless, in fact, had made matters worse. Best leave well enough alone for the time being. Although she was crushed that their promising evening had turned out poorly, she realized he needed time alone.

"Listen, I'm kind of tired. I'm sure you are, too." She jumped to her feet. "Why don't I come back in the morning?"

Clearly troubled, he brushed his hand down his face. "I'm sorry about tonight, baby. Forgive me?"

She reached on tiptoe to kiss his cheek. "There's nothing to forgive."

Brent felt like forty kinds of a fool for letting her leave. But when they made love he wanted it to be perfect. And at the moment he was nothing but an empty shell.

Feeling angry and betrayed, he walked the floor, avoiding the trash can that held his disillusionment. But he hadn't forgotten the letter's message. His life—his trust in mankind!—was falling apart.

Pouring another drink, he swilled it. Loneliness closed in on him. He heard Cella moving around in her kitchen. Cella, darling Cella. God, how he loved her. He ached to race to her arms, to drown in her sweet love.

Suddenly he was terrified. He had pledged love to Marcella Parker, ardent career woman. That realization suddenly overshadowed the miserable truth of the letter.

Brent didn't know what to do or which way to turn.

Marcella fretted over leaving Brent alone with his problems. He needed her, and she had deserted him. Through the night she tossed and turned, worrying over whether or not she should go to him.

With the dawn of morning, her mind was made up. If he wouldn't discuss his inner turmoil, so be it. But she would be there for him when the time was right.

And she had no qualms about her decision of the previous night. She was ready to give herself up to him, to take him into her body, her heart, her spirit . . . forever.

Marcella waited as long as she could, then strolled next door to face a reluctant Brent in his kitchen.

"You heard me. We're not going to waste that picnic lunch I packed," she stated vehemently, hands on her hips, five minutes after she had arrived. "And I'll not hear any more arguments out of you."

"Domineering, aren't you?" he challenged, a slight tease to his voice as he poured two mugs of steaming coffee, then handed her one.

Warming her emotion-chilled hands on the mug, she stepped close to him. "If it gets the job done."

Suddenly she set her coffee on the counter, and reached up to stroke his cheek. "Darling, would big, strong you let poor little me spend Saturday all by myself? I've heard you have a wonderful boat, and I've always dreamed of picnicking on the Gulf."

Brent shook his head, exhaling loudly, and cut his eyes toward the ceiling. Big, strong him? She had a lot to learn. But her feminine charm—or was it blatant sexuality?—had the desired effect. Whatever the case, he wanted to be with her. To hell with the letter's sour statement. He was feeling better already; just being with her made him feel better.

"So you've always dreamed of picnicking on the Gulf," he said while smoothing her hair. "Is this the part where I get to tell you what I've always dreamed of?"

"I'd love to hear your dreams."

"Rest assured, they aren't about picnics."

"Oh? What do you dream about?" she teased. "Hunting? Fishing?"

"Right on." He slanted his face toward hers. "Hunting for you and fishing for your kisses."

"Uh-huh." Smiling, Marcella stepped out of his arms and leaned back on the counter. "I'm not that easy to catch."

"We'll see about that."

The warm salty breeze whipped Marcella's face as Brent's seagoing cabin cruiser headed southwest in the Gulf of Mexico. Land was but a scant line on the horizon behind them. The sky was cloudless, the sun at its zenith. Green water, endless miles of water, surrounded them and protected their privacy. Settling back on the seat, she watched Brent intently. He was a master at the helm.

Clad in black swim trunks of a stretchy material that emphasized his big-boned, muscular physique, he was standing with his feet wide apart as he guided the boat through the cresting waves. The wind whipped his flaxen hair, and black-framed aviator sunglasses hid the faint lines of worry that had branched out from the corners of his eyes. His powerful, bronze-tanned legs were powdered with a fine coating of golden hair, as were his massive arms and broad chest. A lock of hair blew across her face, and she impatiently pushed it behind her ear, wanting nothing to block her view. She wanted his undivided attention. . . .

Her fingers, one at a slow time, wrapped around his wrist. "How about a glass of wine?" she yelled above the engine's roar.

Stopping the motor, he beamed at her. "I thought you'd never ask."

The vessel swayed gently as she made her way to the rear. Brent followed behind her. Heady with anticipation, she sat down on the long bench seat, which ran the length of the boat's open-air aft section, and bent forward to extract wine bottle and glasses from the picnic basket.

"Will you do the honors?" she asked sweetly, offering him the corkscrew.

"My pleasure, ma'am."

And then she set about seducing him.... With deliberate slowness she unfastened her white cover-up. Sliding it first down one shoulder, then the other, she wiggled out of the garment. He dropped the corkscrew and whipped off his sunglasses, and his sea-green eyes scanned her. She wore a midnight-blue one-piece swimsuit. The front veed provocatively low, and the high-cut sides gave extra length to her legs. She noted with womanly delight that his hands wavered as he poured the wine into clear plastic glasses.

Squatting before her, he handed her a glass. "You're beautiful."

"So are you," Marcella said, gazing at her golden god. Attention caught momentarily by the slightly less tan of his inner thighs, she dropped her lashes with sudden shyness. Oh, she would be so very easy to catch....

Grinning, he shifted onto the seat beside her, and in an unexpected move he stretched out on the bench. He settled close to her, and hitching one knee high, he rested his head on her lap.

Her fingers curled into his thick hair, and she leaned to brush a whispery kiss on his forehead. His hand tenderly caressed the column of her throat, the slope of her neck, and a delicious shiver ran the length of her spine. She sighed his name once and then again.

Brent sensed Cella's passionate tremble, and he was overjoyed for it. The light of morning had alleviated his terror of love. He would learn to deal with his apprehension. Somehow.

Staring at her creamy smooth skin and the swell of her rounded breasts, he yearned to pull her into his embrace, yearned to discover just how hard to catch she was. But he wanted to clear the air of the previous night. Before Cella he'd never had the inclination to explain how he felt about his personal or professional life. With her it was different. Further, she had to understand just what kind of a man she was getting involved with. And if she hesitated? He would be honorable. Sweet mercies, he hoped she wouldn't hesitate.

"Cella." His voice was quiet, his expression guarded. "About last night, I owe you an explanation."

"You don't owe me anything, Brent. But if you want to talk, I want to listen."

"Someone, I don't know who, slipped a note under my door. It said—" He cursed lowly.

"What did it say, Brent?"

His voice held a bitter ring. "Sneed Goodman was the original backer for RSK."

"What!"

"He cut a deal with the Corpus Christi bank. Requested that his name be kept out of it."

"But, Brent, why does that upset you? To me it shows that he has faith in you."

"Faith, hell! Faith has nothing to do with it. According to the note, he did it at Vicky's request. Damn her—damn them both! Sneed and Vicky knew making it on my own was important to me. I had half the money needed for start-up, but I was having trouble getting a bank to go along with the other half. I put up everything I own—well, almost everything, but I still fell short. And then the Goodmans took it upon themselves to step in."

"Please don't be resentful." She cupped his face between her palms. "It's obvious that Mr. Goodman still respects you. I'll bet if he realized you need a well-completion loan, he'd be happy to help."

"I will never *ever* take another penny from Sneed Goodman." He wrenched to his feet. His back to her, he stared at the sky. "I'm up against a wall. I can't let my employees down. Their livelihoods depend on me."

She chewed her thumbnail for a second, dreading her next words. "You still have Jerry's partnership offer."

"I'll forget you said that." Brent slammed his fist into his palm. "You can bet your boots Sneed'll know in no uncertain terms to stay out of my business—way out."

"Brent, he won't allow RSK to go under. He'll lose a great deal of money."

"Oh, yeah?" He picked up his glass, quaffing the wine. "The money isn't important to him. He has to consider his spoiled daughter. Blood's thicker than water, you know." His head shook in disgust. "There was more to the letter. It said that after Vicky and I divorced, she told her father to veto any more loans with the bank in Corpus.''

"Oh, Brent, no.''

"I never figured Vicky for a calculating, vindictive person.'' He shrugged a shoulder. "Sneed, either, for that matter. Guess I've learned a lot about human nature.''

"Please don't lose your faith in others,'' she pleaded, desperate to pull him out of those thoughts that had changed his teasing mood.

"It may be too late,'' he said.

"Don't say that.'' Walking over to where he stood, she put her arms around his waist. She felt him quiver as her lips touched his rock-hard back, tasting the salt of his skin. "I believe in you, darling. And I love you.''

He whirled around, grabbing her elbows. His fingers bit into her flesh. "I love you, too. But when and if RSK goes under, how will you feel? I'll be broke, Marcella. Flat broke, do you understand?''

"You won't be flat broke. You'll have me. Wealth doesn't matter to me. I've never had it, so I have nothing to lose.'' She gazed past the strong planes of his cheek, capturing his eyes. "Please don't think about what they did to you, at least for this one afternoon.''

His arms tightened around her, and he held her closely. "Thank God for you, Cella.''

While she was pleased that he had confided in her, Marcella's heart was aching for Brent. His stubborn pride was going to be his downfall, if he let it. She didn't know what more could be said to soothe the blow to his ego. But maybe with her love and loving she could make him forget, at least for the day. And tomorrow? With luck he would see things more clearly.

Brent buried his face in Cella's clean-smelling hair. He thanked his lucky stars she'd come into his life. She was his soul mate, his friend, and she made it easy to forget.

A grin of pleasure played across his face. By damn, she was running her hand down his back, smoothing her palm across his buttocks. She wiggled in that age-old way women had of enticing a man. He felt his desire rise. He wanted to turn fantasy into actuality, to stop fighting and start hoping.

His low laughter was almost a growl. "Woman, are you trying to seduce me?"

"That's what I had in mind," she replied provocatively. "If it's not asking too much."

"I thought you said you weren't easy to catch."

"I lied."

## Chapter Eight

If there was one thing Brent Coulter had learned about Marcella Parker, it was to expect the unexpected. And here on his boat, with the calm of clean air and a cloudless sky, the idea of Cella proving how much *she* wanted *him* was a potent aphrodisiac. Heart doing flip-flops, he watched the sun dance through the midnight highlights of her hair, watched her Wedgwood-blue eyes speak a thousand words of sweet seduction. And her slender hands...oh, mercy, they were smoothing over his pectorals, tangling into his chest hair. But would she have qualms...after?

"Well?" she whispered throatily. Her lips parted— to Brent they were like the beginning blossom of a rosebud, dewy in the spring morning. "Am I asking too much?"

He called up the thin thread of his honor. "Are you sure? You understand how I feel about certain things. I don't want you to have regrets later."

"I'll only have regrets if we don't...."

"Then I think something can be worked out," he teased, his heart as free as the gulls flying above.

Her palm slid to the top of his swim trunks, her pinky playing with the waistband. All at once a swell rocked the boat, and his arms snatched her to him, steadying her. This was the moment he had lived for.

Swooping Cella into his arms, he cradled her to his chest and turned to the cabin door. "I'm *certain* something can be worked out."

Marcella nestled close to Brent as he ducked his head through the hatch and carried her into the cruiser. From the corner of her eye she took in the interior. Polished teak gleamed against monochromatic beige upholstery and green woven pillows. The scent of wax filled the combination galley and salon. Tufted seats were arranged around a small table along the starboard side; galley counters hugged the port. And forward Brent carried her...taking them both to the queen-size bed that reigned over the bow. To Marcella the accommodations were luxurious...and romantic.

Uninhibited, she brushed her lips on the springy hair above his chest, tasted the salt-air tang of his skin. As if she were light as a petal and more precious than gold, he placed her on the bed. Leaning over, he fanned her hair across the pillow and settled beside her.

His big body made her all the more conscious of the differences in their sizes, but she wasn't threatened.

Instead she felt protected and wanted to be covered by his virile strength. As she sighed in contentment, her hands massaged the hard wall of muscles beneath his shoulder blades, urging him to her.

Yet he didn't yield to her unspoken invitation. His mouth dipped to her ear. "Easy, sweetheart, you're all that matters to me, and I want to make this good for you."

"Make love to me, Brent," she pleaded, astonished at her own brazenness.

"I was afraid I'd never hear you say that." His eyes reflected the elation in his soul. Then he aligned his body with hers, his palm stroking her arm. "But, baby, we have all the time in the world."

"What if I can't wait?" Marcella challenged with her voice, her eyes. One hand moved across his jaw; the fingers of the other wound through the wavy hair above his ears. She reveled in those tingling sensations of sun-weathered skin and a million strands of coarse yet soft hair.

"Can't wait, huh?" His low, throaty growl melted through her. His hands pinned her arms, his thighs touching hers as he angled himself above her. "Then prepare to be tortured, little wildcat."

And torture her, he did. Slow sensuous torture that held no pain, only pleasure. His body seemed light, counter to his big frame; he held his weight slightly away from her as if he were frightened of crushing her. But the slight friction of his chest against her breasts made her gasp for more of Brent. Her moan was muffled by his claim on her lips and the ardent yet gentle thrust of his tongue as it deepened their kiss. His fingers wove through her hair, gently tugging, and his kisses of fire burned across her cheek to the side of her nose.

"Close your eyes, baby."

And the flame of his lips flicked first one closed lid, then the other.

"Please," she moaned as his pelvis nudged against her thigh. "Oh, yesss."

Brent was at the brink of losing control. He was aching to possess her savagely, to love her fast and furious and then love her slow and long. But he wouldn't. She was too fragile, too delicate. And to him her satisfaction was paramount. Magic smooth, he unfastened one swimsuit strap at her shoulder, then the other. As he kneeled above her his hands circled her breasts, his fingers drawing the suit down to her waist. Breath catching in his throat, his eyes devoured what he'd only dreamed of before.

"God, you're lovely." Her rounded breasts were milky white and satin smooth, crested rosy and proud. His hands, his mouth, his entire being wanted to know and to cherish those precious mounds adorning his beloved Cella.

Marcella felt Brent's heated flesh touch hers, and she basked in his tenderly aggressive seduction. Her hands held him to her chest as his lips circled and laved and treasured with feather-light touches. She gasped as he feasted deeply, his cheeks tightening and relaxing, over and over. As if in a daze, she cried out his name.

Nothing, absolutely nothing, had ever felt so wonderful, so completely right as when his mouth trailed to her other breast, giving it the same blessed thrill. Then, raising backward, he drew the material from her body. And she lay nude before him, quivering for the fulfillment of his love.

With every beat of her heart she wanted to make him happy, but doubts whipped through her. She wasn't sure she knew how to satisfy him; he was so fiercely male, so passionate.

"Brent," she murmured, "tell me how to please you."

"Just let yourself go, baby, let it happen. That'll please me," he answered adoringly, green eyes devouring blue. He swayed to his feet and pulled his swim trunks down his legs. Bending and balancing first on one foot, then the other, he yanked the garment and threw it over his shoulder. He towered to his mighty height, naked and aroused.

Marcella's eyes widened, and she felt it difficult to breathe. He was beyond beautiful. He was male perfection.

Brent searched her features, looking for signs of fear. There were none. All he saw were the shining features of Cella, waiting to be loved. Oh, God, how he adored her! He wanted only to give, and with his giving he would take the most precious gift of all—the heart's sharing ties. He leaned to trace his fingers along her cheek. "My beautiful baby. My beautiful destiny."

She opened her arms. "Love me, my darling."

Fluidly he returned to her. Never before had lips touched the arches of her feet. Marcella was floating, ascending the heavens as his mustache touched her sensitive skin, his tongue circling her ankle bone. She moaned as his caress continued up the inside of her calf, then brushed her thigh, her hip. His fingers rolled the peaks of her breasts, exerting a pressure that spiraled through her, settling in the nether regions of her midsection. She sighed tremulously as he whispered kisses on her tummy. As his hand settled above her pelvic bone and pushed slightly, his tongue touched her navel in the rhythm of lovemaking.

"No more, oh yes, no," she pleaded, half out of her mind. Her fingers curled into his hair, and her thighs parted. "Now—now!"

He angled his body with hers and captured her lips in a drugging kiss. All the while touching her intimately. She muffled his name, almost in a sob, into his mouth.

"Am I hurting you?" he asked cautiously.

"Nooo. Oh, no!"

He gently circled and tantalized her most sensitive place. Thrashing, she begged him anew to cease his exquisite torment. And yet the thought of him stopping was agony without end.

"Touch me," he ordered, his voice husky with passion.

Sudden shyness overcame her, but she felt the need to know all of him. Her fingertips slid over his hip, then closed around his manhood. A growl vibrated in his chest. His leg, so solid and hairy, settled between smooth thighs. Finally her eyes closed with the pleasure of having him atop her. Lips meeting hers, he groaned her name. Tongue twining with his, she explored the silky recesses of his mouth, loving the taste and scent of him.

"Look at me, Cella," he whispered, pulling away to look deeply into her dilated eyes. "I've been dying for this."

"Then this must be heaven."

"Tell me, Cella. Tell me!"

She needed no explanation. "I love you, Brent."

A strong shudder of elation rolled through him. He underlined his words with feeling and sincerity. "I love you, Cella."

And then the torture was over. No, it was only beginning, she realized as he slowly claimed her. Nothing in her past experience had prepared her for the exquisite sensations that assailed her.

Brent whispered encouragements into her ear, then bowed his head to kiss her lips, then her breasts. Sweet mercies, he was aching in his efforts to be tender!

"Don't hold back," she pleaded, her pulse thumping in rhythm with his thundering heartbeat. "Don't hold back."

The last of Brent's bridled control slipped. Catching her hips in his powerful hands, he surged, full and hard, into her. She answered with the arch of her hips and the twining of her legs around his back. With every mighty thrust he branded her his...and his heart was seared forever with her being. Her hands explored his back, then dug into the flesh of his shoulders. He gritted his teeth, aching to bring her to passion's sweet climax before losing grip on his own excitement.

Then after kissing her ardently he whispered, "You're driving me insane."

Eyes closed, her breath rushed in and out. Wave after wave of sweet sensations washed over her, as surely as the cresting ocean beat against the boat's hull. And she craved more of Brent, as if she couldn't get enough of him.

"Oh, baby, I love you," he groaned.

Hearing his impassioned voice, his heaving breath, his echoing heartbeat, she was ecstatic that she could bring him to such fervor. In this wondrous, delicious rapture a tide of passion peaked within her—an awareness she'd never felt before. As her nails dug into the flesh of his hips, her body quaked at the pinnacle of human emotion.

Then all his senses accelerated as he poured the essence of life into her body. And as she took his precious gift she knew if death had called at that moment, her life would have been complete.

"Are you hungry?" Brent asked as the sun began to settle in the west.

"For what?" Marcella returned in a teasing voice, nestling against his chest. Spent, they lay face-to-face on the cabin's bed.

"Woman, have mercy on this poor weakened soul!" He clutched his naked stomach, feigning starvation. "I meant food, as in sustenance to the body."

"I'm not a bit hungry for...food."

"Too bad, you insatiable wildcat. I am!"

Brent planted a quick kiss on Cella's forehead, then lunged to his feet. To keep from crawling back into bed and making love with her again, he pointedly didn't look her way. There was time for that later, he reasoned while tucking a towel around his hips. Moving aft and onto the deck, he grabbed the picnic basket, neglected hours earlier.

He recalled her seductive overtures; they had been a swift antidote to his problems. Never in his wildest imagination had he expected the fire of Cella's sensuality—or his, for that matter. They had spent the afternoon talking and caressing, whispering and loving.

In the afterglow of their expressions of love, he was totally fulfilled, as never before. In the past he'd had more than his share of women. Looking back on those times, he guessed that he'd been caught up in the technique of what a woman expected during sex. But with Cella giving pleasure wasn't technique; it was the act of love.

When he fell for Vicky he had tried to please her. Of course she'd never put forth any effort to seduce him—ever! He strongly suspected he'd never truly loved his ex-wife, not like he did Cella. That might have been part of their problem.

No words could describe the genuine love he felt for Cella. Beyond that—far beyond that!—he was touched that she had put aside her mistrust and placed her faith in him.

And those precious gifts had made him forget, at least temporarily, about his disillusionment over the Goodmans' double-dealing. Suddenly their betrayal didn't have the impact it had before.

Happier than he'd ever been in his life, he started back to the cabin.

Marcella basked in his adoration when he returned to her side. By the fading sunlight filtering through the portholes, Brent fed her bites of cheese; he held the wineglass to her lips. She relished each sip, each bite with an "mmm." But she was really relishing his tender attention, the musky scent of his skin and the way he crooned sweet words into her ear.

Would she awaken later to find this was only a wonderful dream? Please don't let that be, she prayed. Brent roused her in ways she'd never imagined. He made her feel as if she were the only woman on earth. And to her he was the only man who had ever lived.

His thumb wiped a trace of wine from her bottom lip. "He was a fool."

"What!"

"That guy who broke your heart was a fool, Cella." His hand caressed her arm, her shoulder, the column of her throat. "But it's his loss. You're my woman now, and I don't intend to ever let you go."

"What do you mean?" she asked hopefully, guardedly.

"You heard me. I want to fall asleep in your arms and wake up to your loving. And in the evenings I want it to be you and me. That is, if that's what you want, too."

*He wants to marry me!* In not so many words he'd proposed. This was the happiest day of her life!

Marcella's hands cupped his face. "Nothing would make me happier."

He moved against her, his need pushing against her flesh. "Want to seal the bargain?"

"I can't think of a better way...."


The next morning Marcella awoke in her bedroom with the solid form of a sleeping giant pressed to her back. Easing out of Brent's arms, she turned to him. A smile lifted her mouth as she watched him sleep. His mane of hair was tousled. The tiny lines of worry that had creased his face since he received that anonymous letter were gone. While his large frame seemed incongruous in her frilly four-poster, somehow it was right for him to be there. Lord, how she loved him!

Mona Lisa jumped to the bed, curling against the crook of Brent's knees. A loud purr vibrated as the cat rubbed the side of her face against his leg. Marcella stifled a chuckle. She and the feline had been two crabby spinsters. But both were changed through the love of a good man.

Marcella was tempted to wake Brent, but decided to let him rest. She figured he would be hungry as a bear; he had a voracious appetite... for many of the essentials of life. As quietly as possible she pulled on her robe and closed the bedroom door behind her.

Coffee dripped in the maker, its aroma enticing. The kitchen table was set. Humming a nameless tune, she whipped up a hearty breakfast of ham, soft-scrambled eggs and hashed brown potatoes. Her pet was treated to a can of mackerel. Sipping a mug of eye-opening coffee, she popped four pieces of bread into the toaster.

"You broke your promise," Brent said in a raspy grumble. "Why'd you leave me?"

"Good morning." Grinning, she turned to the man who sounded like a woebegone little boy. Mona Lisa pranced over to him and braided around his ankle. Coffee mug suspended in midair, a shiver of delight raced through Marcella. "I thought you'd be starved."

Brent leaned against the doorway, stifling a yawn with the side of his fist. He wore only burgundy briefs, which accentuated his tall, powerful body—and the bold maleness she now knew well. Obviously enjoying her slow perusal, he stretched out the kinks in his muscles. The thought of seeing him like this every morning made her hand shake in anticipation, and coffee sloshed to the floor.

"Yeah, I'm starving all right." His hand brushed across the morning stubble that shadowed his jaw. Then pushing away from the jamb, he strode to her. He took the cup from her hand and placed it on the counter behind him. She went into his waiting arms. "Do I get your seal of approval?" he asked, kidding her.

"I think you'll do quite nicely."

"Is that all you can say? 'Quite nicely'?"

She smiled up into his face. "Mr. Coulter, are you fishing for an attaboy?"

"Yep."

"Well, then—attaboy!" Swatting his taut backside, she moved back. "Now sit down, you big beautiful beast," she ordered, "and eat your eggs."

"Cella, the dominatrix," he ribbed, obeying her orders. Then on apparent second thought he stood and seated her. His palms smoothed down her arms, then cupped her breasts. "Must say, though," he whispered in her ear, "you're quite nice yourself." The emery roughness of his chin moved across her cheek. "And you raise mighty appetites in this beast."

Hand still shaking, she picked up her napkin. "I'm famished—for food," she stated, stressing the last word. If he continued with his caresses, well . . . Smiling, she turned her face up to him and batted her lashes. "You wouldn't want me to perish, would you?"

"Woman, you drive a hard bargain."

Sitting across from her, he dug into his breakfast with zeal, complimenting along the way. They chatted amiably, with the ease of two people accustomed to one another. Despite Marcella's assurances that Mona Lisa had been fed, he dropped morsels to appease the cat's culinary alms-seeking meows. Polishing off his third cup of coffee, he patted his lean stomach.

"If you're gonna cook like that all the time, Cella love, you can—" again patting his middle "—kiss this goodbye, I'll be fat as a hog."

"I'll try to find something to like about you," she razzed merrily.

If he were hairless, toothless and weighed five hundred pounds, she would still love him. He stole a piece of toast from her plate, and she adored the easy familiarity of the action.

"Of course, after we're married, I'll have you on tofu and water...."

The toast in his hand dropped to the table. Brent's face blanched, ashes of yesterdays crowding his mind. This was déjà vu. He had played this scene with Vicky. Strength left him as he settled back on the chair. "Married?"

Arranging her fork carefully next to her place, Marcella seemed to study the table edge. "I thought you wanted to marry me," she murmured brokenly.

"I'm sorry...." Apparently he'd given Cella the wrong impression. As much as he loved her, he wouldn't be caught in another no-win situation. Rising to his feet, he went around the table and hunkered down beside her. He took her cold hand in his. "I'm not ready for marriage. I thought you understood that."

"B-but after...after yesterday and last night, I thought—" She twisted away. "What did you mean by waking up next to me and all that business?"

"We can live together. That way we'll find out if we're really compatible."

She pulled her hand from his. "You misled me, Brent."

"Not on purpose. I thought we were on the same wavelength. I want a commitment, and I thought you did, too."

With dull wariness Marcella regarded Brent. His offer was a page from yesterday. Jim Turley had never asked permission in plain English to move in with her, but his belongings had arrived bit by bit in her apartment. Asking and implying were basically the same thing on the bottom line, she concluded, and the results were bound to be the same—heartbreak. Whatever the case, she absolutely, positively would not take that chance again.

"Well, what do you think?" he asked, sliding his arm across the back of her chair.

"I do want a commitment. But I won't settle for that type."

"Don't dismiss it out of hand. Living together would be devotion and companionship and a union of our souls. What more can you ask of a commitment?"

The truth of his statement whipped through her. He had a point, but she would not leave herself open for another disappointment. She blinked back the burning sensation in her eyes. "A lot more. Things like working toward the same goal of building a life to-gether, raising a family and appreciating each other as we grow older.''

"And you think a piece of paper is going to guar-antee that? Cella, I've been married—it doesn't.''

"But doesn't a religious and legal pledge make a person think twice when the going gets rough and the temptation is great to say 'to hell with it'?''

"Yes," Brent admitted slowly. "But we've only known each other a few short weeks. For God's sake, let me get used to the idea of being in love. It's going to take time to find out if I can deal with your career. Vicky put her job before me and before everything else. I'm not going to lie to you; I won't put up with that sort of a relationship in the future. I know that sounds selfish, but that's the way I am. That's why we need to see if our love is strong enough to withstand the test of time.''

"Am I always going to pay for what your ex-wife did to you?" She had to know. "You told me you love me. And I love you. Can't you bury your doubts?''

His features turned grim. "I had three miserable years married to a woman who held her job higher than me.''

Marcella pushed herself away from the table and made for the living room. "And I had six miserable months living with a man who had no intention of marrying me.''

"It looks like we both have ghosts to fight. Neither of us trusts ourselves to go the extra mile.''

"I think that about sums it up," she said.

"Then forget I asked." Walking up behind her, he pulled her to him. "We'll work it out, baby. Someway."

"I hope so."

He squeezed her arms gently and dropped his chin on her shoulder. "I've got to make a trip out to the rig. Please go with me. We can talk."

Unable to face drilling rigs in the best of times, she uttered, "That is the last place I want to visit."

"I know you're angry and hurt, Cella, and I'll give you some time."

"I'd appreciate that."

He dressed and left.

Minutes later Marcella stood under the shower head and let the hot, stinging water beat down. Why, oh why, didn't love ever work out right? she asked herself.

She had jumped into a loving relationship with Brent without really thinking through the consequences. Wasn't that to be expected? Love *is* blind. After he had admitted his love, she was ready to throw inner doubts to the wind. Plus her hopes had been buoyed when he'd hinted at what she thought was a proposal. She needed to come to grips with the fact that marriage might never be a part of their future. And that burned through her soul as hotly as the stinging water beating down on her back.

She fought for rationality. Perhaps she had jumped to conclusions about a live-in situation with Brent. Just because Jim had broken her heart didn't mean Brent would do the same thing. And she realized that her feelings for Jim couldn't be compared to the all-encompassing love she felt for Brent. Back then she had been in love with love.

And she realized despairingly, she and Brent had more than the ghosts of past relationships to fight. While those problems could be worked out with love and patience, Brent also had a hang-up about her career. Though she loved him with all her heart, she was not going to run scared about her livelihood.

She, too, needed time to regroup.

Brent rushed back to the duplex from the Rollins Field as quickly as possible. Though he'd botched the morning, he felt good. Being in love was the greatest feeling in the world. But he should have handled Cella more carefully. She had been shocked when he had blurted out his hesitation about marriage. That was to be expected.

Marriage was still o-u-t, he reaffirmed. But he had no one to blame beyond himself for their quarrel. He should have said point-blank what he meant about "later regrets" before they made love.

He would make it up to her. With any luck they'd kiss and make up, enjoy each moment as it came—and worry about the future in the future.

Cella's sedan was pulling out of the driveway. In a fast move he blocked her departure with his Bronco and jumped from the cab.

Dressed in a baby-blue jersey top, white cotton skirt, and heeled sandals, she bounced out of her car and stomped toward him, her ponytail swaying from side to side.

"What do you think you're doing?" she asked testily as he strode to her.

"Oh, I don't know." He hoped light banter would break the ice. "How does making a citizen's arrest sound?"

She rolled her eyes. "Spare me."

"Where're you headed?" he drawled.

"Antique auction."

Marcella was set on putting some distance between them, which was difficult considering how much she loved him. But she needed to keep away, at least until she could sort through her emotions.

He stepped closer. "I'll go with you."

"You'd be bored stiff."

"Cella, I'm sorry about this morning. You caught me off guard." His palm brushed her cheek. "No, don't turn your head—look at me. That's better."

Her eyes scanned him. He looked like a million dollars, even though his clothes were casual: Levi's, a plaid cotton shirt and rough-out boots. A slight breeze ruffled his thick hair, and his eyes were as bright as the sun reflecting off the sea. His finely sculpted mouth twitched momentarily, then widened into a smile that unveiled his even white teeth. Wanting to be with him, she felt her resolve weakening.

"My job is as much a part of me as you are," she blurted.

Appearing to study the concrete driveway, he dug the tips of his fingers into his front pockets. "I know."

"I don't know how to deal with your hang-ups about my career. We need a cooling-off period, Brent, and I think we shouldn't see each other for a while."

His clear eyes settled on her uncertain gaze. "If we waste the present, we're lowering the odds of having a future."

"You're right." Marcella swallowed hard. "Would you really like to attend the auction with me?"

"You'd better believe it."

When they arrived at the auction house, Brent stayed outside to smoke a cigarette while Cella browsed through the displays. Heaving one more sigh of relief that she had given him time to deal with his mixed emotions, he visualized her. Damn, she made him feel good! Missing her presence, he finally joined her.

He draped his arm across the back of her chair. His field of vision swept the crowded room. An assortment of men and women vied with enthusiasm for the wares of a wizened, bald-headed auctioneer and a not-too-snappy helper.

This was not Brent's idea of fun. If Cella would pay a little attention to him, it might be all right. But she didn't. He might as well have been invisible. He guessed she wasn't quite over their tiff. Well, he would try to make the best of being here.

The auction recalled his mother's penchant for antiques. He thought of the dreamy look in her eyes when she'd brought home a "find." That look ran counter to her usual crusty personality. The only other times she got that expression was when she gazed at his father.

Cella's knee brushed against his.

"How about a Coke?" he asked, hoping to get her attention. No answer. "Cella, are you deaf?"

"What?" She continued to look at the auctioneer as though he were going to disappear if she quit watching him.

"Never mind."

She turned her face to Brent. "I'm sorry, honey. What did you say?"

"Cella, this stuff is junk," he stated. "How much longer are you planning to stay?"

"A few minutes longer," she replied impatiently. "And it's not junk. Antiques have character and history."

"Never one of my better subjects," he said lightly, thankful for the opportunity to talk. He squeezed her shoulder, pulling her against him. "You know, you sound like my mother. She's always poking around these sales."

"Then we'd get along famously." You've never asked me to meet her, she didn't add.

"Yeah, probably." He shifted on the too-small folding chair. "Let's go out of here and go fishing."

Visions of his living room bedecked with a varnished marlin, glassy-eyed moose and bodiless deer formed in Marcella's mind. "You'd rather murder a poor little fish than sit here?"

"Yes."

"Number seventy-one, folks," she heard the auctioneer call.

Marcella faced forward, intent on her purpose for being there, everything else forgotten. She was on pins and needles for item seventy-two, her prospective purchase for the day, to come up for auction. Of course, almost everything had great possibilities. A little glue here, a lot of paint remover and stain there— oh, the possibilities were limitless, she figured, visualizing the finished products.

She stole a glance at Brent, who was making a big show of boredom. Chances weren't good that she could interest him in the hobby that had filled many of her lonely hours.

Well, you can't have everything, she surmised optimistically. Their hobbies and interests were totally opposite. In the past she had wanted a life partner who would share her interests. Now that was no longer of prime importance. She shouldn't have made that crack about murdering fish. That had been crass. The main thing was to interest Brent in *her*.

"The next item, number seventy-two, is a fine walnut Victorian cradle, folks." The slight man knitted his bushy brows and turned to a strapping assistant. "Steve, get that thing over here!"

The young man wet the tip of a pencil with his tongue and then made a note on a clipboard.

"Steve, did you hear me?"

"Yes, Poppa." With a slowness uncharacteristic of an auctioneer's assistant, Steve set the cradle on the block next to the podium.

Marcella's voice held reverence. "Isn't it beautiful?"

She pictured the unusual cradle refinished, polished and with an embroidered mattress cover resting next to her bed. It would make the perfect sleeping haven for Mona Lisa.

"Whaddam a gonna hear for it?" The auctioneer scowled. "Come on, folks, let's get the bidding started! Do I hear ten?"

Marcella was a seasoned auction hound. To test the waters she let the uninitiated start the action. The bidding rose quickly in five-dollar increments to forty dollars, then died down. A good sign. Still she didn't raise her numbered paddle. The white-haired man, wearing a taxicab-yellow Hawaiian shirt, two rows in front of her waved his hand slowly. She'd watched him. By his cunning bids she pegged him for a dealer.

"Do I hear fifty?"

"Oooh, it's a steal," Marcella whispered, raising her paddle in the air.

Brent's eyes rounded in horror. What in the name of hell was she planning to do with a crib? She had her mind set on wedded bliss; but if she was planning to catch him by way of a shotgun barrel pointed down his nose, she should be more subtle.

He leaned closer to her. "Cella—"

"Shh!"

She continued a bidding war with a fellow in front of them.

"Marcella, you're not planning to fill that thing, are you?" Brent asked bluntly, not to be put off.

Features clearly showing distress, she turned her face to him. Her arm dropped, and she placed the paddle on her lap.

"Sold to the gentleman in the yellow shirt," the auctioneer intoned. "Get that pencil outta your mouth, boy, and take down his number."

Marcella swallowed the lump in her throat. Realizing how bidding on a cradle must have appeared to Brent, she blinked away the burning sensation in her eyes. Then anger surfaced. She flounced to her feet and made her way down the crowded aisle. After dropping the paddle on the registrar's desk, she hastened outside.

"Cella?" Brent's hands tightened around her arms.

She rounded on him. "Yes, I have plans for a cradle."

His hands fell away, and he looked as if he had been struck.

## Chapter Nine

Brent squared his shoulders, towering beside Marcella in the auction-house parking lot, deserted except for automobiles. "Are you trying to trap me into something I don't want?"

"Don't flatter yourself. I'm looking for a cat bed, not a *baby* bed!" Marcella straightened to her full height, bound and determined not to be intimidated by Brent. Her hopes and dreams shriveled within her. "Let's cross our fingers no unwanted complications have already begun."

His face went ashen.

"And what if they have, Brent?"

"I'd do the right thing."

"But you wouldn't like it."

"No, I wouldn't like it."

Her fists tightened at her sides. "Don't worry, I won't saddle you with a child you don't want."

"Don't take my words out of context. I didn't say I wouldn't want the child. How could I not want a product of our love?" He rubbed his brow. "What I'm saying is that we have to come to grips with our differences before we get locked into something that would tie us together for a lifetime."

She backed away a step. "Chances are slim that I'm...pregnant. This isn't the right—or should I say, wrong?—time of the month."

"We'll have to be more careful in the future."

"Oh, we'll be more than careful. There's only one absolute way to guarantee there'll be no *misconceptions*—abstinence!"

"Don't be irrational, Marcella. There are other ways, good ways."

"I won't take the chance." Her eyes felt scratchy and dry, her throat swollen with unshed tears. "After my mother died when I was a baby, my father raised me single-handed. It wasn't easy for him. I won't even go into the effect it had on me." She hugged her arms and headed for his car. "I wouldn't put my child through the same thing."

After yanking the door handle, she slid onto the seat. She wouldn't cry! To allow him to see how deeply he had hurt her was unthinkable.

Easing into the car, Brent cast a look at Marcella. Head turned to the side window, she hugged the armrest. Their "reconciliation" had turned out all wrong. *Me and my big mouth.* He slipped his prescription shades past his temples. His handling of the matter had been as myopic as his eyes.

The car hummed along the highway. Cella didn't speak to him. He didn't blame her. Sure, he deserved her anger. A lump suddenly formed in his throat as he envisioned being married to her and having a houseful of children. He had never given much thought to fatherhood before. With Vicky it had been a foregone conclusion that offspring would complicate her climb up the corporate ladder. He'd been agreeable.

But the idea of having a couple of miniature Cellas was growing on him. Of course genes have a tendency to get all mixed up. He grinned. He and Debbie were prime examples of that. It had turned out all right for them—he was tall like their mother and Debbie was a shrimp like their father. Aw, what would it matter if he and Cella ended up with a six-foot daughter and a five-two son? he asked himself. He would love them. And the world could always use more models and jockeys. Or better yet, the wee one could follow in its father's footsteps.

He stole a glimpse at her once more. Did she look like her mother, her father or maybe a grandparent? Well, whoever she got her looks from, they must have been good-looking.

If she was pregnant he wouldn't shirk his responsibilities. Matter of fact, he looked forward to the prospect. And to be honest with himself, marriage—with or without the issue being forced—might not be so bad.

"I've been thinking. If we are to become parents, I'm going to train our kid, whether it's a boy or a girl, to be a wildcatter. That is, if you have no objections.''

''A wildcatter!'' She glared at him. ''Over my dead body.''

''Okay, okay. You can teach the little nipper to count change at the bank.''

''Just-just, oh, Brent, please leave me alone.''

The bottom of Brent's fist slammed against the steering wheel. Okay, if that's the way she wanted it. He wouldn't give her the satisfaction of knowing how close he was to a total commitment, at least not at that moment. He still had his pride.

Marcella was thankful Brent left her alone the rest of the day and night. Not only had she given her heart to a man who didn't want marriage, she had fallen in love with a wildcatter, who was much the same as her father: dedicated to the oil field. Why hadn't she given that a thought before? Brent Coulter had the power to destroy her.

Perhaps it would be best to make a clean break with Brent, she decided later that next day. Her worries about a child had been pacified in nature's way that morning. At least her mind was eased on that subject. Though she wanted to avoid Brent, she was obligated to tell him that no complications had arisen from their lovemaking.

After leaving the bank that afternoon, she didn't find Brent at home. She steered her car toward the headquarters of RSK Petroleum Corporation. His convertible, as well as Debbie's and Jerry's cars, was parked alongside the building. There would be no privacy. Should she return home and wait for Brent?

No, he might drive out to the rig. She would ask him for a few private minutes.

When she walked in the office, Brent was ranting and raving to his sister and to Jerry Hagen.

"Clear out," he ordered heatedly, pointing a finger at first one employee, then the other.

Debbie's lower lip pouted. "Gosh, Brent, I don't know why you—"

"Debra, did you ever hear of respect for authority?"

"Come on, Deb," Jerry put in, grabbing her arm. "How 'bout an ice-cream sundae?"

"With chocolate sauce and sprinkles?"

"'Course."

"Mmm, that does sound luscious." Debbie stuck out her tongue. "Good night, Marcella. Sweet nightmares, *Lefty*!"

Quiet settled through the office. Brent's arms were crossed over his chest, and his spread feet were planted to the floor as he glowered at Marcella.

"What are you doing here?" he asked.

"I have something to tell you." Marcella turned away from his angry visage. "Brent, about . . . about yesterday—"

"Yes, about yesterday." He walked up behind her and squeezed her shoulders, pulling her against him. His voice lost its grating quality. "I'm sorry about everything."

"You can breathe easier. I discovered this morning there's no baby." She was glad her back was to him, and she wouldn't have to see his look of relief.

"Oh."

That simple word sunk through Marcella. He had sounded—sounded *what*? Why, he sounded disappointed! If she lived to be a hundred, she would never understand him. Or herself. But she'd said her piece; it was time to leave. "That's all I came here to say. I'll be going now."

"Don't go, Cella," he said raggedly, his breath fanning against her ear. "I need you."

"No." Moving away, she turned. "I wasn't joking yesterday about no sex."

"That's not exactly what I had in mind." His voice was heavy with longing. "But I won't deny I need you that way, too."

A shock of sexual electricity arced between them. Tiny bumps rose on her arms. Why had she drawn that line between them? She wanted nothing more than to be in his arms once more. "What . . . did you mean?"

The galvanizing charge was broken as Brent evidently remembered his former frame of mind.

He brushed his hand down his face. "The Railroad Commission served notice on me today. They're shutting down the well."

No matter what her personal feelings were, it was impossible not to sympathize with his plight, and her heart went out to him. "Oh, no."

"Oh, yes. Nevill Rogers isn't convinced I have the money to keep up my lease payments."

She sank onto a chair. "Surely something can be done."

"I've talked to Rogers and the RRC till I'm blue in the face." Walking the length of the office and back again, he ran a hand through his hair. "I've got to find a way out of this bind."

Marcella felt terrible about her part in his problems. If only she hadn't returned RSK's checks that day, how different everything would be! Hindsight's twenty-twenty, she thought regretfully. There was nothing she could do about that mistake but try to set matters right. She had a professional obligation to Brent.

She went to his side, taking his icy-cold hand. "You'll find a way. And if you'll allow me, I'll help you."

"No, I'll handle it myself."

"But you said you needed me."

"Your presence and friendly ear, that's all."

Be patient, she ordered herself. And patience it took as she attempted to penetrate his stubbornness. But slowly, as the minutes passed, Brent seemed to warm to her reasoning.

Cella was nothing if not persistent, Brent realized as he listened to her sensible arguments about her willingness and ability to use her professional expertise to help him. It eased his tension. To hell with Rogers and the RRC, at least for the time being.

She was standing close to him, her blue eyes bright. He could smell the sweet scent of her perfume. She looked beautiful in that dove-gray sheath dress, he noted. She always looked beautiful. But her beauty went beyond the exterior.

He didn't deserve her. He'd behaved like a jerk the day before, at her house and at the auction. How this woman could be understanding of him was a miracle.

"All right, partner. We'll work on it together," he acquiesced, moving to take her in his arms. "Seal it with a kiss?"

If his lips touched hers, would she be able to live up to her convictions? Marcella felt apprehensive about the corresponding qualities between Brent and her father. While it would be self-destructive to continue either platonic camaraderie or a sexual relationship with Brent, she loved him. Loved him! She was not going to let the aching memories of her father's demise keep her from the man she adored.

"One kiss—that's all," she finally answered.

"Agreed."

His hands cupped her derriere, bringing her closer to him as his lips found hers. Feeling her strain on tiptoes to lace her arms around his neck, he lifted her to him. She tasted of mint; she was warm and womanly. A groan vibrated from his throat as he kissed her thoroughly.

When their tender embrace ended, he looked at her with love written across his features. "Cella, I'd like to take you home to meet the folks."

Her smile touched her eyes as elation soared through her. Brent wanted her to meet his parents!

"Want to meet them, Cella?"

"Nothing would delight me more," she replied, flattening her palms against the warmth of his shirt.

"They're gonna love you!" He led her to a chair, then dropped to the cracked Naugahyde, pulling her onto his lap. She moved from him, but his grip stopped her. "The old man'll think you're gorgeous and sexy." A warm callused finger gently swept a wisp of hair from her temple. "And Mom'll think you're 'sweet as a peach.'"

She felt him grow hard against her hip. He rubbed her bottom lip with a light and sensual touch. Breathing was next to impossible as a thread wound through every vein, every nerve in her body to remind her of how marvelous it felt to have him inside her.

"Sweet as a peach?" she repeated, trying to ignore her wanton needs.

"That's her highest seal of approval." His hand brushed across her breast, moving in slow, circular patterns. "God, how I want to make love to you."

Her voice was shaky. "Brent—"

"How about next Friday, then?"

She scooted to her feet. "Not Friday, not ever."

"I meant to meet my parents."

"Oh. Friday," she repeated dully, looking away. "Can we make it Saturday instead?"

"No way. My parents're leaving for the Bahamas on Saturday. Besides, Mom's got the menu planned out for Friday. I promised her we'd be there."

"Oh, Brent, I can't."

His brows knitted as he drew back. "Why can't you?"

"Sneed Goodman's planned a dinner Friday for the Chairman's Council, the bank's wealthiest depositors," she explained.

"I know that. I got an invitation. But what's the dinner got to do with you?"

"I'm expected to attend."

"Dammit, tell Sneed you have other plans."

"Be reasonable, Brent. It's an opportunity for me to get to know my customers personally."

Brent reached around for a package of cigarettes lying on the desk. He felt sapped of strength as he dug in his pocket for a match. The match blazed to life, the tip giving off the slight smell of sulphur after he snuffed its flame. That's how he felt: like a burned-out match.

Inhaling a deep lungful of smoke, he watched her. She clutched her arms, and her head was bowed. To a certain degree he understood where she was coming from. He knew he was being selfish, but he couldn't stop himself from asking, "That's your final answer?"

"If I had a choice I'd go with you to your parents' home. But my first consideration has to be my job. It's my livelihood."

"And it's more important than us?"

"Don't be a hypocrite, Brent Coulter. I wouldn't ask you to turn your back on a professional obligation."

"I'll make excuses to the folks," he said slowly, and wheeled the chair toward his desk. "Look, I've got a lot of work to catch up on. You can identify with that...."

"Yes. I'll be going."

Staying busy after she left was no problem. Letters to Nevill Rogers and to the RRC were written out in longhand, then stacked on Debbie's desk to be typed.

Cella had been gone about thirty minutes when he stretched his tired muscles, then stood to pace the linoleum floor. He didn't want to think about Marcella, but he did. They had hit another stalemate in their relationship. Why had he let himself fall in love with another career woman?

Bruised personal feelings aside, Brent still had business problems to deal with. He appreciated the fact that Marcella was eager to spend time helping him find a way out of his predicament with the government people. But even if they found a successful solution, he still needed money. Badly.

He smoked cigarette after cigarette until his throat was raw while considering his options. He had checked out the banks in Houston; they wanted more collateral. The deal with Hagen was out; RSK was Brent's company, and he intended to keep it that way. Selling the boat would bring in some ready cash, but a sale would take time he didn't have. He had a couple hundred thou in cash left. That would still leave him short.

There was only one thing left to do: go for his ace in the hole.

He dropped onto his chair. Resting his elbows on his knees, he rubbed his eyes with the heels of his palms. The only viable solution was to mortgage the ranch. A bitter taste rose in his mouth. He had sunk to the bottom. The Crooked Horn had been in his mother's family for six generations.

Brent's maternal grandmother passed away the year before and had willed him the place, had expected him to keep the property in the family. And now he was forced to jeopardize the land and a century and a half of family tradition.

But what pained him the most was the effect it would have on his mother. Lois Coulter took pride in her heritage. She'd seen fortunes come and go with his father. Her son was determined to protect her feelings.

He was certain that the Rollins Field would become a high-yield producer. Of that he had absolutely no doubt. Two years earlier Brent had played the petroleum landman, scouting through old records and doing a lot of tedious research. The day he discovered a yellowed document tucked away in a courthouse vault, he knew where his first exploratory well was going to be drilled.

Nevill Rogers's ranch sat above a huge pool of oil, and the cantankerous rancher knew it but had kept the knowledge quiet. He was old school. Before Brent had talked him into leasing his mineral rights, Rogers had held on to the outdated Texas tradition of cattle and oil not mixing.

But Brent hadn't counted on how many lengths of pipe and megabucks it would take to get to that reserve.

One more thing was certain. He wouldn't let word get back to his mother that he intended to mortgage the Crooked Horn. Ever. Best not tell anyone, including Cella—she was too close to Grand Canyon-mouth Debbie.

Brent decided to leave for Houston the next morning, after a few hours of shut-eye. He wouldn't go home; sleeping in his office chair was preferable to being only a wall away from Cella. That was more than he could handle right then.

Marcella felt terrible about letting Brent down. But what was she to do? To disregard Sneed Goodman's invitation would be folly. She had an obligation to the depositors who made her paycheck possible. And looking back on that first day near-disaster over RSK's account, she was in no position to put her pleasure ahead of her job.

For what seemed like hours she drove her sedan through the deserted streets of Port Merritt, then along the coast highway to Corpus Christi. For some reason she didn't want to go home to four lonely walls or to chance seeing Brent. Her equanimity couldn't handle another run-in with him.

Hunger pangs gnawing at her stomach, she searched for a respectable-looking eating establishment. To no avail. Finally she parked the car alongside two eighteen-wheel semis at a truck stop under a red neon sign flashing "Eat!"

Marcella smoothed the skirt of her dress before entering the fluorescent-lit café. Two men wearing Stetsons, apparently the truckers, sipped coffee at the Formica counter, which had a glass cabinet holding an assortment of pies. The men gave her appreciative glances, then returned to their conversation. She walked to the far corner and slid into a booth, turning from the greasy, fly-specked window.

A curvaceous brunette waitress waltzed up. The woman set a glass of water and a slick, vinyl-covered menu before Marcella.

"Evenin'." She smiled pleasantly. "Cuppa coffee?"

"Iced tea, please. And a cheeseburger, well done."

"Mind's made up, huh?" The waitress chuckled and dug a napkin-wrapped knife and fork from her gingham apron, placing them on the table.

"Yes, it is."

No, it wasn't, at least about her personal life. While waiting for her food Marcella commiserated over her problems. The bone of contention between her and Brent was her career. And just when she could have shown him that he was the most important thing in her life, she'd let him down. For crying out loud, what had gotten into her? Getting on a chummy basis with her customers could certainly be accomplished without attending the Chairman's Council dinner!

By letting her career stand in the way of her future with Brent, she was making a terrible mistake. Could a job hold her and love her and make everything all right? Of course not! And she remembered the disappointed sound in Brent's voice when she had told him she wasn't pregnant....

She would meet Brent Coulter halfway.

No longer hungry for anything except Brent's love, Marcella handed the waitress enough money to cover her bill and a tip and left. The wheels of her car couldn't turn fast enough as she raced back to Port Merritt.

To Marcella's disappointment, Brent wasn't home when she arrived back home. Evidently he was still at his office, or perhaps he'd gone to the rig. She decided to wait for him at home.

The next morning his car was still missing. She thought of leaving a message on his telephone answering machine. No good. Remembering the day that seemed so long ago, she walked outside her house and gathered a bouquet of wildflowers from the field adjoining her yard.

She filled a porcelain vase with water, then arranged the flowers prettily. Placing them on his garage doorstep, she leaned a note card against them.

"What time Friday night? Love, Marcella."

And then she traveled to Goodman National, where she told Sneed Goodman in no uncertain terms that she would be unable to attend the upcoming dinner.

Brent whistled "Dixie" Wednesday evening. A wilted buttercup was pressed inside his shirt pocket for luck and to remember the woman he loved. He stepped on the gas, hurrying back to Port Merritt, making a quick detour by his folks' house. Thoughts of the past few days were at the forefront of his mind.

The outcome of his trip to Houston appeared positive. He'd reapplied for a loan, using the ranch as collateral. The bank planned to send an appraiser to the Crooked Horn, but word was his loan application looked good.

Hell, everything was looking good! After finding Cella's bouquet he'd been on top of the world. What a woman! he thought happily, for the thousandth time.

Ma Bell was going to be pleased come billing date. Brent had called Marcella numerous times over the past two days, chatting for hours. His only regret was the necessity of wooing the Houston bankers. It kept him from what he wanted most: to be with Cella.

He'd done some serious thinking during their time apart. On all levels—mental, physical and emotional—he yearned to share a life with Cella. That meant unequivocal commitment. But marriage no longer frightened him. In fact it was a challenge he looked forward to.

He had been a fool to equate Cella with Vicky. They were as different as night and day. His darling wasn't selfish with her time and love by any stretch of the imagination. Cella knew how to balance a career and a personal life, and he would never come up lacking.

She had the right to pursue her career; she'd worked hard for it. And their future children wouldn't lack for love and motherly attention. If she wanted to work outside the home, he had no doubt the quality of the time she spent with the little ones would make up for the quantity.

Yes, Marcella Parker was one career girl worth the chance.

Marcella dropped her needlework when she heard Brent's car pull into the driveway. Racing to the mirror, she finger-combed her hair and smoothed her siren-red silk nightgown—bought for his homecoming. She had given up on her pledge to keep Brent at arm's length, had seen a doctor to take the proper precautions.

Throwing open the door, her heart raced. Brent's fist was poised in midair, apparently ready to knock. A grin of pure delight played across his lean features.

"Hello, baby," he whispered in a tone that was wickedly suggestive.

Her voice matched his in temper. "Hello, yourself."

With a force that left her breathless, he swung her into his arms, then kicked the door shut with his foot.

"I've been lonesome for the woman I love," he admitted with a gentle roughness. "I don't know if I can keep my hands off you."

"Then don't." Her eyes locked with his. "Make love to me."

He nearly dropped her.

"Am I hearing right?"

"Everything's . . . taken care of."

His eyes flickered for a brief moment. "Guess that's smart."

"Are you going to stand here holding me all night, or are you going to take me up on my offer?" she asked, smiling.

He grinned mischievously. "Sure you don't need to take care of your cat? Hmm. Maybe I should spring Fred from the kennel...."

"Brent!"

"Impatient, huh?"

Quickly closing the distance to her bedroom, he shouldered the door open and placed her on the bed. The buttons were practically ripped from his shirt as he undid it, then yanked the garment away.

"Who's the impatient one?" she ribbed.

"Both of us."

Her heart beat wildly in anticipation as he unsnapped the top fastener of his trousers and pulled down the zipper. She flexed her hands, aching to touch him. In one fell swoop he slid trousers and briefs from his tall form. And her arms beckoned him to her. She would love him and not worry about whether he loved her enough to spend the rest of their lives together.

"I'm getting very impatient," she whispered seductively.

"Hussy," he growled, smiling as he moved toward her.

Marcella sighed as the mattress sagged under his muscled weight. Straddling her body, his mouth dipped to her throat—teasing, nipping, taunting. She squirmed beneath him. He lowered himself, his weight not allowing further movement. The need within her cried out for him.

His finger stroked her bottom lip. "I love you, Cella."

"I love you, too."

Their lips met, and her thoughts and doubts were washed away as she gave herself up to the passion that overwhelmed her. Deftly he slipped the nightgown off, tossing it away to lay crumpled on the floor, and aligned his body with hers. She quivered at the feel of his crinkly hair on her sensitive skin. She cupped his face between her hands and delighted in his rapturous attention. Savoring the clean taste and masterful touch of his lips, she deepened the embrace. She was drowning in a sea of erotic fascination. Once, and then again and again, she purred his name as he stroked her flesh. And then their hands, their lips, their entire range of senses devoured and adored each other, as if their separation had been years, not days.

Her fingers laced his thick hair as he cherished her breasts. A velvet cord of heightened ecstasy wound and tightened through her, demanding to be assuaged by his total claim to the rights she offered.

"I have to know all of you," he demanded, a deep timbre in his tone.

His lips trailed lower to explore and tantalize each cell in her being. Words of love, like wisps of smoke, told her of his adoration. And then...oh, then, he tasted her as if she were a delicacy too long denied. Her head thrashed from side to side as she reveled in this new experience. Alive with the mélange of emotions stirring within her, she cried out in a daze of passion. Sliding his body over hers, he possessed her fully.

"Tell me you love me more than anything else in the world."

She repeated the words that sent him into a glorious frenzy. With each hard thrust of his manhood, she ached for more. Spinning, whirling, climbing higher and higher, she moaned her love. Hearts beating, racing as one, they scaled the heights of ecstasy to its devastating summit.

Minutes later, their flesh hot and musky in the afterglow of fused spirits, he whispered, "I've waited a lifetime for you."

"And I for you," she murmured, her eyes closing as she snuggled against his warmth. Somehow she had to forget that a lifetime was only to last until he tired of her. She gave herself up to the solace of sleep, where doubts and uncertainty were swept away.

Brent cradled Cella's head against his chest. His life was complete. Nothing mattered but her. With his love by his side, he could face any problem.

He kissed the top of her shampoo-scented head and watched her. Asleep, she didn't stir. But he couldn't wait a minute longer to pop the question. Reaching over the side of the bed, he grasped his trousers. His fingers closed around a small velvet box.

Shaking her lightly, he blew into her ear. "Hey, sleepyhead, wake up."

She wiggled her naked body against him. "Nooo, wanna cuddle."

His hand stroked her firm flesh. "Wake up. If you want to marry me, you'd better wake up!"

## Chapter Ten

*I must be dreaming.* And Marcella didn't want that image to drift away. Half-asleep, she tangled her leg around Brent's calf, tugging the sheet around them.

"Yes or no?" he asked huskily, pulling the sheet away, then moving to brace his hands on both sides of her body. "Do you or do you not want to be the mother of my children?"

His words registered, really registered, and she smiled up into his face. "Are you sure? What made you change your mind?" she asked carefully.

"I wanted to ask you before we made love, but I guess I got caught up in the moment."

She felt the warmth of his skin against her. More than that, she sensed the ardor of his words. And she realized that his offer of everlasting commitment came from the depths of his soul. "Oh, darling...."

Slow as treacle his sun-browned hand rose in front of her. Then, even slower, he turned his palm up and spread his fingers. A black jeweler's box rested in the callused center.

Her heart skipped a beat, and she was speechless.

"Aren't you going to open it?"

With trembling fingers she took the case from his hand, and fumbled with the top. Set in a filigree mounting, an exquisite emerald surrounded by round-cut diamonds twinkled in the lamplight, shooting brilliant flashes of light.

"It's beautiful!" Her smile was as bright as the ring. "Is it an antique?" she asked, wondering why she'd asked an immaterial question when she should have been saying yes to his proposal.

"Darn right it is." He lifted the ring from the box. "It belonged to my grandmother. She willed it to me with the proviso that I give it to the woman I intended to spend the rest of my life with."

"You didn't offer it to Vicky?"

"No, Granny passed away after my divorce." He held the heirloom to the tip of her left ring finger. "You're the woman for me. Am I the man for you?"

"Yes." She felt the pressure of the gold as it slipped past her knuckle. "Yes, a million times over, yes!"

He kissed the underside of her fingers, then guided her hand over his shoulder. "Here's to the future, sweetheart."

And he made love to her tenderly, reverently, thoroughly. Together they spiraled in unison to *petite mort*, the ultimate height of loving satisfaction. Her euphoria knew no boundaries as she finally slept, content not in a dreamworld, but in the wondrous reality of their future.

Marcella's alarm radio blared at seven sharp. She shut it off quickly. Too bad. Another workday. Rising to a sitting position, she crossed her arms and laced her fingers languidly. Birds sang good-morning from outside her window. Dawn filtered lines of sunlight through her bedroom's miniblinds. Oh, to heck with Goodman National Bank!

"Mrs. Brent Coulter," she whispered. The sound of it was lovely!

As she turned to look at her fiancé, Marcella's grin widened. Brent's eyes opened slowly, watching her. His fingers curled around her forearm as he leaned to kiss her elbow. Her pulse quickened at his knowing touch, and tiny flesh bumps rose to tell him what he did to her.

"Morning, almost-wife," he whispered in a sleep-roughened voice, catching her into his arms. "I feel wonderful. I love waking up next to you."

"Mmm, the feeling's mutual, my love." The hair on his chest tickled her breasts, and she shivered in anticipation. "Brent, I have an engagement gift for you."

"Not again," he groaned with mock exhaustion.

"What if I begged?" she joked, thumping his ribs.

"I might be able to *rise* to the occasion."

Rolling her eyes, she shook her head. Leaning over to the bedside table, she opened the drawer and pulled out a small flat box.

He took it from her hand, his fingers lingering on her wrist. "What's this?"

"You'll have to find out for yourself."

A silver lighter nestled in the crushed velveteen.

"Thank you, baby. It's super. What made you decide to buy me a lighter?"

"I didn't buy it. It was my father's."

"Your father's?"

"Yes. I want you to have something that's precious to me, something money can't buy. Just like your grandmother's ring."

He touched her cheek, and his voice was tender. "Oh, baby, then I'll always cherish it and the spirit it was given in."

"Then how about a thank-you kiss?" she challenged, watching him test the keepsake, sans cigarette.

He set the lighter on the nightstand and slid his arms around her. "You mean like this . . . or like this . . . or like this?"

She was tingling from his kisses to her lips, her throat, her breast. "No, like this," she answered, aggressively taking over as she made love to him.

Much later, in the warm luster of the aftermoments, he spoke. "You're going to be late for work."

His reminder brought back her earlier decision. "Guess what!"

"You've won the Irish Sweepstakes?"

"Better than that. I've decided to play hooky today."

Eyes wide, he slapped his forehead. "Am I hearing right? The dedicated financial wizard is going to play hooky?" His countenance expressed befuddlement. "Something's wrong."

"Nothing's wrong!" She batted her lashes, Southern-belle style. "Let's go swimming." She sang out the last word, throwing her hands in the air.

Brent braced his neck with his hands, lying back on the pillow. "No can do." He thrust an elbow in her direction. "You can play hooky, but I can't. I'm the boss, remember?"

"You'd rather go into the office than be with me?"

"Of course not. I've got to check on the rig, and I'm going to take you with me."

She touched the ring, new on her finger, as she might stroke a talisman. "I'm worried about you."

"Now what?"

"I'm afraid you'll get hurt or—" She couldn't verbalize the word *killed*. "I'm afraid there'll be an accident."

"I'm not reading you."

"If I lost you like I did my father, I wouldn't have any reason to go on."

"Cella, you're borrowing trouble."

She bit her lip, turning away from him. "You never had your father die in your arms."

He pulled her close. "Baby, I'm not going to deny that accidents happen in the oil field. But think about this: your father was a roughneck. He was on the job for hours at a time. I'm management. My physical contact is minimal out there. I'm not going to get hurt."

She wasn't entirely convinced. "But—"

"No buts about it." His voice took on a solemn quality. "Every moment counts in this life. For a while I forgot that myself and almost lost you when I let my past muddy up my thinking."

"But it terrifies me to think about going to the rig."

"That's exactly why I'm taking you. We've decided to spend the rest of our lives together, and you're going to conquer your fears."

"Maybe another time," she said raggedly.

"No, dammit, today."

"I won't!"

She did—with reluctance. Brent gave her the grand tour of the site; the tour he had wished for back during her first day at the rig. They started on the ground; he explained the workings of the huge centrifugal pump, which stood next to a reservoir of drilling fluids.

"When we're 'making a trip,' like we are right now, the mud hog pumps fluids through that steel-reinforced hose—" he motioned with one finger to the hose connecting pump to rig "—to the swivel and down through the kelly joint and drill pipe to the bottom of the well." He continued to explain the full process. Then, evidently, he noted her confusion. "This oil field jargon's on the boring side." He winked. "I'll shut up and introduce you to the crew."

"Maybe just a little jargon at a time, and I'll be able to absorb it."

"You gotta deal."

He took her elbow, and they climbed the stairs to the rig floor. He introduced her to the crew, reacquainting her with the tool pusher—his poker pal, Frank Hocker—and explaining various safety precautions.

On one hand, her heart was singing. She was confident of Brent's love and commitment. On the other hand, she couldn't put aside her apprehensions, which seemed to echo in the dark clouds hovering above. But maybe she was, as Brent had warned her, borrowing trouble.

When Frank involved Brent in a lengthy technical discussion, she made her excuses and descended the iron-grid stairs to the ground. Doffing Brent's extra hard hat, she turned it around and smiled. Soon her name would be Coulter.

A streak of lightning zipped through the overcast sky, and she cringed. Stepping backward, she glanced up at the rig. Brent didn't appear the least concerned about the inclement weather.

He walked around the rig floor, the tool pusher in tow. Above the roaring diesel engine and the turning rotary table, she heard Brent's hearty laughter. Her chest tightened. He was in his element; this was the life he loved. His work meant as much to him as banking did to her. Somehow, someway she would learn to live with it.

Tires squealed to a stop behind her. Waving at Jerry Hagen, she strolled to his car. He returned her greeting and scooted his wiry frame out of the vehicle.

"As I live and breathe, it's Marcella Parker!" He planted his hard hat atop his carrot-red hair. "How ya doing?"

It was on the tip of her tongue to blurt out the wonderful news about the engagement, but she decided that announcement should be made by both her and Brent. "I'm fine. And you?"

"Fine, fine, just fine." He gave her a friendly mock clip to the arm. "In a hurry, though. Got to talk with the cap'n." He started to walk away, then stopped, turning, and tilted his head toward her. "Why aren't you at the bank?"

She grinned shyly. "I decided to spend the day with Brent."

"My stars! Getting along that good, huh?"

"*Very* good."

Winking, he shot her a salute. "That's the best news I've heard in a long time."

*Me, too.*

He started up the stairs, but halted when the maintenance engineer shouted from beside the mud pump.

"Hocker, the mud hog's shimmying—we got problems!"

Jerry flew down the stairs and ran toward the engineer, who shot over to the auxiliary pump and attempted to get it in operation.

"Stay back, Jerry!" she heard Brent yell as he took the steps at a fast clip, jumping over the railing near the ground. Frank Hocker was right behind him.

"Nooo." Marcella stepped forward hesitantly, her hand flying to her mouth.

A boom rent the air as an impeller exploded through the housing, shrapnel bursting and propelling.

"Awwwgghhh!" Jerry's body shot backward from the impact to land in a crumpled heap. Blood gushed from his shoulder.

"Stop drilling!" Brent and the tool pusher yelled at the same time, unnecessarily.

An emergency horn blared repeatedly, competing with the rolling thunder that crashed through the air. Sheets of rain suddenly began pelting everything within seeing distance.

In a flurry, Marcella went to the injured geologist, kneeling beside him on the soggy ground and cradling his head. The maintenance engineer—miraculously uninjured—raced over, but left again to attend the disabled pump. In a daze, Jerry shook his head. Desperate to keep him still, she steadied him. A river of crimson flowed over her engagement ring.

"We've got to stop the bleeding," she wailed to Brent, to the gathered drilling crew. "Get a cloth for his wound!"

Jerry's voice was weak. "I—I'm o-okay."

"Lie still," Brent ordered, yanking off his shirt and handing it to Marcella. "Call an ambulance, Hocker, and get the first-aid kit. You men step back, he's being taken care of."

She folded the shirt quickly and pressed it against the torn flesh. The shirt and her hand were soon covered with dark red blood.

Each minute dragged out like an hour as they administered aid to the fallen man. Raindrops mixed with Marcella's tears of helplessness and frustration. To Marcella, each fraction of a second recalled that day many years earlier when her father had lain mortally wounded.

At long last the ambulance screeched to a halt beside them and the attendants took over for Marcella and Brent. Hugging her arms, Marcella watched the man and woman team as they placed Jerry on a stretcher and loaded him into the emergency vehicle. With siren blaring and wheels cutting through the soggy turf, the ambulance headed toward the hospital.

Marcella's attention was riveted to Brent. His broad shoulders, always before lofty and resolute with confidence, were now hunched in emotional agony. Brushing moisture from his face, he focused on her. His expression mirrored her anxiety.

"Cella, about the accident— Please don't make too much of this."

But she did. Marcella realized her glorious plans for the future were now in ruins.

While the crew stayed at the rig ascertaining damages, Marcella and Brent traveled to the hospital. Antiseptic smells stung Marcella's nostrils. A bell pinged from the nurses' station down the corridor. They were alone in the emergency waiting room. Clutching her upper arms, Marcella shivered as she leaned against the wall.

"No word yet, Hocker," Brent responded into the pay telephone. "They're working on him now. Yeah, I'll let you know as soon as we hear something." He paused. "Did the maintenance engineer get the backup pump on line? Good. Drilling's started? How's the downhole pressure? Good, good."

Marcella grimaced. The well. Always the well. She shivered again.

Brent replaced the receiver and, striding to her, shrugged out of the lightweight jacket he'd found in the back of his Bronco. Neither had spoken a word beyond Jerry's welfare since the accident.

"Here, take this." He fitted the coat around her shoulders.

Unable to meet his eyes, she fixed her gaze on his muddy, blood-encrusted Levi's, then upward to his bare chest. "You'll be cold," she said dully.

"Coffee'll cure that." He ambled over to a vending machine and dug coins out of his trouser pocket. "Black?"

"Yes, please." Her teeth were chattering. Not from the chilly air or her still-damp clothing, but from nerves.

"Let's sit down," Brent suggested, inclining his head toward a bench along the wall. She walked to the seat and leaned against the wall, closing her eyes.

"Cella, we have to talk."

Wearily she brushed her tangled mass of hair away from her cheek. "You don't want to hear what I have to say."

He blew steam from the paper cup. "I'll have to hear it eventually. We might as well clear the air right now."

She set aside her coffee. "Rig accidents *do* happen to management."

He exhaled loudly through his gritted teeth.

"Brent, for us, for our future children, give up the oil field."

"You can't mean that!"

Her tone was harsher than she'd intended. "I want to be a wife, not a wildcatter's widow."

Brent took a long time to answer. "I can't give up my company. That's asking too much, Cella."

Anger born from fear billowed in a red mist before her eyes. "You're just like my father. He didn't love me enough to give it up, either."

"That was a low blow."

"You have to decide, Brent." She underlined each word for clear understanding. "It's the oil field or me."

"I'd do anything else in the world for you, but I can't give up what I've worked all my life to attain on the outside chance that I might get hurt."

"Or killed."

"Or killed," he admitted. "Cella, it's the quality, not the quantity of life that matters. You can't live your life in a vacuum. People are born, and people die. But between that time, with any luck, they find love and happiness. Life doesn't hold any promises, and chances have to be taken. If not, there's nothing meaningful between being born and dying."

"Don't do this to me," she pleaded.

"For God's sake, baby, we could walk out of here and get hit by a truck or something and be killed. Rigs aren't the only places accidents occur."

Marcella realized the truth of his words. Yet she couldn't let go of the past. She would not allow herself to relive through Brent the nightmare of losing her father.

"This is my second experience with a rig accident, Brent. I guess I'm superstitious, but bad things come in threes."

They stared at each other. And from the look on his face, the winner was clear. Marcella had lost. She had asked for more than he was able to give.

The wide swinging door opened. A green-clad doctor walked toward them. "Mr. Hagen's going to be fine. The injuries aren't serious. He'll be sore for a while, but nothing's broken. We've cleaned out the wounds and stitched up the lacerations in his shoulder and arm. But we'll keep him overnight to check for a concussion.''

Brent and Marcella breathed sighs of relief in unison.

When he started to put his arms around her, she backed away and reminded him to telephone the drilling crew. Watching as he leaned an elbow against the wall while speaking with total concentration to the tool pusher, Marcella realized that nothing could mend the wounds in her heart.

Brent was oil field, her mind told her heart. From her father, she had learned that once petroleum beats through a man's veins, nothing was more important. If they married she would be in constant fear of losing Brent as she had lost the only other man she'd ever truly loved.

On the drive back to Port Merritt, she carefully avoided eye contact with Brent, who tried to start conversation. To no avail. Almost as soon as the car stopped in front of their duplex, Marcella rushed inside, locking the door quickly. Staying next door to him was impossible. What could she do? A motel. That was the answer. She threw clothes in a suitcase and shoved a protesting Mona Lisa into the cat carrier. She had to flee from Brent—and from herself.

When Brent heard Marcella's car pull out of the garage, his heart nearly broke. Wearing a trail in the carpet, he searched for answers. He didn't know how to deal with her; she had drawn herself into a shell.

He lit a cigarette and choked on a swallow of smoke. Damn! Why had the accident happened on the day of their engagement? Timing couldn't have been worse. Would he ever be able to convince Cella to take a chance with him? But he had to be optimistic. Perhaps time would ease her misgivings.

Why had the accident happened in the first place? *Coulter, mishaps happen on rigs, you know that. All the safety precautions in the world aren't going to stop them.*

Thankfully this one was minor in damages. Jerry would be all right; he was a tough hombre. What about the next one?

Should he give up RSK? Brent agonized. If he did it would be like cutting out a vital element of his being. His work was as necessary to him as breathing. But Cella was just as important to him. What was he going to do?

As the days went by Brent's misery accelerated. Cella didn't return to her duplex. He tried to phone her at Goodman National. Each time Sharon made excuses for her boss. He mulled over confronting Cella at the bank but decided against it. Obviously she needed time to adjust to the latest turn of events.

In the meantime Jerry Hagen was released from the hospital to convalesce at home. Through the geologist Brent learned that Marcella had brought a large supply of home-prepared frozen dinners and other foodstuffs to the geologist. She'd stayed to chat and attend to the recovering man's comforts. Brent asked him to find out where she was staying.

According to Jerry, Marcella clammed up when any mention was made of where she was hiding out. Time and again Brent drove by every hotel and motel within an hour's drive. He didn't find her.

By late Friday afternoon he'd had enough. Intent on not giving up on her, he vowed to confront Marcella come hell or high water. And he needed her now more than ever.

The elderly bank guard, Horace Simms, was turning the lock on the door as Brent approached the building. After waving in recognition Simms let him into Goodman National. The two men said their hellos, then Brent started toward Cella's office. The lobby was deserted of customers, and the tellers were tallying their receipts.

Mouth drawn in a waver-thin line of disapproval, Bernice Prothro stomped toward him. "Bank's closed."

"Hello to you, too, Bernie."

"What are you doing here?" The head bookkeeper sniffed while watching him with a knowing expression. "The Chairman's Council dinner isn't until eight, and it's being held at Mr. Goodman's house."

"Excuse me." He sidestepped her and strode toward his mission. What made her think he was going to the dinner? That didn't matter. Bernice always looked for trouble, probably thought he hadn't gotten an invitation, and just wanted to turn the screw.

"Um-hmm. Going to see Ms. Parker, aren't you? Everyone knows the two of you are as thick as thieves," he heard Bernice say from over his shoulder. When he didn't reply, she went on. "You know, Brent Coulter, I never did like you. The high-and-mighty Ms. Parker, either."

To the best of his knowledge, Bernice Prothro didn't have benevolent feelings toward anyone.

"The two of you deserve each other," she muttered.

Turning slightly, he grinned as he responded to her last statement. "I certainly hope so."

## Chapter Eleven

Body tensing, Marcella heard the deep, resonant sound of Brent's voice outside her office. She had done everything she could think of to avoid him. But during their separation he had never left the forefront of her mind, nor had the mud-pump catastrophe. Though she wanted to forget the accident, her perspective was awash with the fear deep-seated in her psyche.

Yet, knowing that Brent was within feet of her thrilled her no end. Brent was perfect for her. Except for that one flaw, which wasn't a flaw in his character. It was her own.

He pushed open the door to her office and strode in, closing the door forcefully behind him. "I can't go on like this," he uttered hoarsely, his gaze colliding with hers.

"Me, either," she returned, meaning it, but refraining from rushing to him as she collected her wits.

"Do you still want to be my wife?"

"With all my heart. But after..." Unable to go on, she looked away. The silence deepened, then she studied his tormented face again. "But, Brent, I meant what I said. It's wildcatting or me."

"My fondest dream is to make you happy." Stepping closer, he brushed his hand across his mouth. "I have an idea. I'll make arrangements to hire someone to take care of my responsibilities. I promise you, I won't get within a hundred yards of the rig unless absolutely necessary."

She shook her head slowly. "Brent, that's a noble concept, and I appreciate your trying to go fifty-fifty, but hiring someone to do your job is unworkable."

"You're right. It was a shot in the dark." He leaned over her desk and took her hand. "We're going to work it out. Someway. But just as you can't give up your career, I can't give up mine."

She pulled her hand from the tight pressure. "Then it won't work."

"Don't say that." He peered with anguished eyes at her. "We have to give it time. Didn't time take care of my doubts about your job?"

"Yes," she admitted. "But how much time?"

"As long as it takes. But, baby, I'll try my damnedest to find a solution. Take a gamble on us."

While Marcella had never been one to rely on twists of fate, she knew that nothing short of a miracle would change Brent's line of work.

But whatever the future held, too much was at stake for her not to take the gamble. They had buried their past emotional hurts, and Brent had learned to accept her career; they had a future together. She wouldn't give up the love they shared.

"Tonight's the night you're supposed to meet my folks. When we leave there, Mom and Dad are going to know I'm going to be your husband. Are you agreeable?"

"Yes, my darling."

He rounded her desk and pulled her into his arms. When they stopped kissing to start breathing, he buried his face in her hair. "I love you," he murmured.

Arm in arm they left the bank. On the way to the Coulter's home outside Port Merritt, Brent was uncharacteristically quiet. The hushed atmosphere gave Marcella a moment in which she remembered the events of her workday. Darn! How could she have forgotten to mention meeting Nevill Rogers?

Just as she opened her mouth to speak, Brent beat her to the punch.

"We're here, baby." He smiled his slow grin and reached for her fingers. "They're gonna love you."

Brent whipped his convertible to a stop in the circular drive fronting his parents' home, and a shaft of light instantly shot from the front door. The Coulters hurried from the house to the car. Brent's father opened Marcella's door, ducking his head inside the auto.

"Welcome, Marcella."

The genuine warmth of Albert Coulter's greeting was echoed by Lois Coulter as she led them to the house. Brent's parents came pretty close to the way Marcella had pictured them—with the help of Debbie's earlier description.

Brent was the spitting image of his mother. Mrs. Coulter cleared six feet easily and was rawboned. Her son had inherited her facial bone structure, as well as her height. Her hair, lighter than Brent's, was streaked with becoming touches of gray. If Brent aged with the grace of his mother, he would be an awesomely appealing middle-aged man.

Albert Coulter moved with the speed and frame of a bantam rooster. His eye color, evident behind glasses, had been passed down to his children. Springy salt-and-pepper hair crowned his sun-weathered, friendly face.

Whom would their children resemble? Marcella wondered as she gazed lovingly at Brent. She hoped they all looked like, well, any of the Coulters.

"You two rustle us up some cocktails," Brent's mother ordered with authority as she slipped her arm through Marcella's. "I'm going to show Marcella around the place."

After they had toured the sprawling one-story, Marcella said, "Your home is lovely." She hoped her words hadn't had a sycophantic ring.

"Now, girl, don't be just saying that."

"I'm not." She grinned at the older woman. "I'm partial to antiques, too."

"Ladies, drinks are served," Albert announced, handing them both a martini.

Brent slid his arm over Marcella's shoulder, hugging her to him.

Winking at Marcella, Lois sidled up to her husband. "You can't beat old relics for durability. My Albert here's like fine wine; he improves with age."

"Now, honey bun, you're embarrassing me." He didn't look the least bit embarrassed.

Judging from the tender yet sparking looks passing between Brent's parents, she saw they obviously still adored each other, even after many years of marriage. Marcella smiled shyly at Brent. *I'll bet you'll be like fine wine....*

After dining the four of them savored brandy-laced coffee in the spacious oak-paneled den.

"Your roast beef dinner was delicious, Mrs. Coulter," Marcella complimented earnestly, no longer worried about the impression she was making—the Coulters made her feel at home.

"I second that." Brent patted his stomach, leaning back in an antique rocker chair opposite the sofa, where his mother and Marcella sat. Leveling an appreciative glance toward Lois Coulter, then smiling at Marcella, he said, "Cella's a great cook, too."

"Best way to a man's heart," Albert added smartly, waving a cigar in the air. "Caught me, didn't it, honey bun?"

"Hush, Albert, you're going to embarrass the children." Now it was Lois's turn not to appear at all embarrassed.

When Brent said, "I'm already caught," three sets of eyes honed in on him. He walked to Marcella, gently pulling her to a standing position. His arm slid around her waist as he faced his parents. "I'm going to marry her."

Pandemonium reigned. Except for Marcella, everyone spoke at once. Brent's father crushed her with his congratulatory kiss. Mrs. Coulter—after insisting that Marcella call her Mom—squeezed both of Marcella's hands.

Looking her up and down, Lois grinned broadly. "Son, you're a lucky man. She's sweet as a peach."

"What did I tell you?" he whispered in Marcella's ear.

"Have you set a date?" his parents chorused.

"That's up to Cella."

Marcella was sailing on a magic carpet of happiness as the evening progressed. She was overjoyed by her acceptance in the Coulter family circle. At long last she would be part of a family.

"Albert, come help me with the dishes," Lois ordered, tolerating no argument.

"I'll help you," Marcella offered.

"Daughter, your day'll come in my kitchen," Brent's mother replied, winking. "Albert, let's leave the children alone for a few minutes." Lois flipped a switch on the stereo as they left, and soft music filled the room.

It was only the two of them . . . alone.

"I've been lost without you. I missed everything about you, baby." Shortening the distance between them on the sofa, Brent turned his face to Marcella. "I get drunk just being with you. I want to make love with you and hear you moan my name when you're past the brink of this world." He paused but for a moment, and his low chuckle was almost a growl. "Aw, baby, I'm going crazy for you."

A tingling sensation assailed her, winding her into his bewitching web. He had the most wicked ability to rouse her with no more than words. His arm tightened around her shoulder, and his free hand slid past her skirt hem and up her thigh. Lips parting slightly, he started to kiss her. Her fingers moved across his mouth, stopping him.

"Brent, don't." Pink stained her cheeks as she realized how much she wanted his caress. "They might come back in."

"They won't." Brent's mustache brushed against her cheek. "Mom'll keep Dad occupied with dishes and taking out the trash."

"Which is exactly what I intend to do with you, Brent Coulter, after we're married," she remarked, giddy with love and alcohol. "Keep you busy in the kitchen."

"I accept the challenge." He paused. "I've got a better idea. We'll get a maid to do the work, and we'll concentrate on making babies."

"Not a bad idea." She looked deeply into his eyes.

"Let's set a date. How about tomorrow?"

"No," she replied sorrowfully, "not until we work out our differences."

Breaking visual contact, he rubbed his neck. "You may have won by default."

"Default?"

He stood, moving to the empty fireplace and cocking his palm against the mantel. The toe of his boot kicked against the hearth. "The Railroad Commission shut down the Rollins One today."

Marcella's heart went out to the man she loved, in spite of her personal fears. Hurrying to his side, she vowed silently to forget the nightmares that plagued her. She had to be strong for Brent. She couldn't lose faith—somehow, someway, a miracle would occur.

Her hands reached to cup his face. "I won't let you down, my darling."

"I hope I won't let you down, Cella."

"Brent? Marcella?" she heard Albert Coulter say from the darkness of the adjoining dining room. "Mind if I come in?"

At Brent's assurance, his father walked into the den. "Something wrong, son? You're white as a sheet. Marcella, you're not backing out on him, are you?"

She squeezed her beloved's hand. "No, I'm not backing out."

Lois Coulter rubbed lotion into her hands as she joined the threesome. "What's going on?"

Brent's admission came out in a rough, emotional voice. "I've got problems with the Railroad Commission."

"I can relate to that. Those old boys have given me more than my share of headaches in the past." Clicking his tongue, Albert poured four shots of whiskey, handing one to Marcella, then one to Brent. "Drink up, children, it may be a long night."

Brent swallowed the liquor that burned a trail down his esophagus to his stomach. He knew that if RSK was dead in the water Cella would be pleased.

Following his parents and a somewhat weaving Marcella to the round table in the corner, he wondered where the family conversation would lead. He wasn't certain that he wanted to discuss his business complications with his father. Albert Coulter was no paragon of petroleum-industry advice. Yet Brent felt the need to share his inner doubts with the ones he loved most.

Albert plunked a fifth of Jack Daniels in the center of the table. "All right, son, what happened?"

Slowly, hesitantly, Brent relayed the events leading up to the Railroad Commission's decision, omitting Marcella's part in the dispute.

"I told you I'd help you, sweetheart," Marcella said, then hiccuped. "I talked with Nevill Rogers today."

Shocked, Brent focused on her. Even after she had told him that it was the rig or her, she still planned to help him? He hoped it wasn't liquor talking.

A grin lit Brent's face. "What did he say?"

"He's a stubborn man," she replied, picking up her whiskey glass.

"I told you so. Aw, hell, even if he dropped his case with the RRC people, I need operating capital."

"But, sweetheart, with the rig shut down, you won't have to pay the drilling contractor." Throwing her hands in the air, she laughed giddily. "Then you'll have time to rob a bank or something for money!"

"Daughter, can I get you a cup of coffee?" Lois asked.

"Oh, no. I'm not finished with my drink."

"I can see you're a woman of your own mind. Like myself, I might add," Lois said smugly, then turned to her son. "We'll help you with money."

"More than happy to, Brent." Albert squeezed Marcella's hand. "Your fiancée has a point. A little downtime's to your advantage."

Brent gave her an appreciative once-over. "Yeah, she's a smart woman."

"How much upfront money and royalty interest did you offer Rogers?" Learning it was one-eighth, Albert clicked his tongue again. "I think I know a way to help you."

"How's that?" Brent asked warily.

Albert poured another round. "Send him a cashier's check for fifty thousand bucks and a new leasing agreement that'll give him a sixth."

"Is that legal, Dad?"

"Damn right it is! Good business, too. Been many a time that I've wanted to use that angle, but I didn't have any money to do it with. Never had anyone to turn to for cash." He leaned to cuff his son lightly on the jaw. "Boy, I'm flush right now. I'll give you the money."

"Thanks, but I don't need it. I can handle the fifty thousand."

"Then let's drink to your success!" Albert exclaimed.

Brent held his glass aloft. For thirty years he had looked upon his father as a failure. Now, with new insight, he realized how naive he'd been. Albert Coulter was a shrewd oilman, a victim of a few bad breaks. Brent could identify with that. He understood his father as never before. Yes, the complication was a blessing in disguise.

Standing, he walked around the table to his father. He intended to do something that was a long time overdue. Embracing his father, Brent said with a husky pitch to his voice, "I love you, Dad."

Albert's eyes shone. "I love you, too, son."

Both men opened their arms to their women. They formed a circle of love. But as Brent held tightly to their touch, he knew that he still had to deal with the biggest problem of his life.

What was he going to do about Cella's adamant opposition to his livelihood?

That night Marcella was plagued with hellish nightmares—screaming bodies flying through the air and rivers of blood coating everything. She awoke shaking in the twin bed opposite Debbie.

A fog of past-night memories waved through Marcella's mind. Brent's sister had returned from a date and had offered to share her bedroom. The teenager had received an if-looks-could-kill glare from her brother. Marcella couldn't remember anything beyond that. After getting drunk during her first meeting with Brent's parents, how was she ever going to face them? She would have welcomed the earth opening and swallowing her up.

Recalling her nightmare, Marcella cringed. After Brent had arrived at Goodman National she had been besotted first with his presence, then with alcohol. Practical reason had vanished. Furthermore, she had promised marriage without any emotional considerations settled—not only in private with Brent, but in front of his family. And even after he'd made it clear that he was not going to give up the oil field, she had offered to continue assisting in his quest.

Her hand trembled as she reached for the glass of water sitting on the bedside table. Trying to wash out her furry tongue, she pondered her predicament. Oh, Lord, what was she going to do?

"Yuck," she muttered, unintentionally splashing water on her arm.

Yawning, Debbie opened her eyes and stretched. "Hi."

"Good morning," Marcella returned, gathering her clothes from a nearby chair.

"Welcome to the family, Marcella."

Her reply lacked spirit. "Thank you."

Trying to disregard her throbbing, boulder-size head, she pulled on her clothes. She would have to face the music. Running her fingers through her hair, Marcella headed for the Coulters' kitchen.

Lois Coulter hummed gaily as she arranged a tray of seltzer tablets, coffee and tomato juice. "Good morning, Daughter."

Marcella's cheeks matched the juice. "Morning." Marcella sank onto a kitchen chair. "This may sound a little made up, but I don't remember much of what happened late last night. I'm thoroughly embarrassed."

"Don't be." Lois plopped two tablets into a glass, brought the fizzing mixture to Marcella and patted her arm lovingly. "We Coulters can handle our booze. I guess it's the old pioneer Western stock in us."

"You may find this hard to believe, but I don't make a habit of getting inebriated."

"You don't need to make excuses. Drink up! That's a good girl," she cooed. "You were flying mighty high last night, Daughter. Brent volunteered to put you to bed—isn't he a darling?—but I shooed him to his own room." Lois smiled with motherly warmth as she set juice and coffee on the table. "Dad and I have to run, or we'll be late for our plane." She winked an eye. "Finally talked him into a second honeymoon—not that we haven't been on one all our married life."

"You're a very nice woman, Mrs. Coulter."

"Mom," she corrected, moving to hug Marcella. "Don't ruin my reputation with that kinda talk. I'm just an ol' country girl who loves seeing her younguns happy. And I'm happy as a clam you're one of them."

With that Brent's mother swept out the back door. Gulping the refreshing liquids, Marcella shriveled inside. Why did Lois Coulter have to be understanding? Why hadn't she looked down her nose at her? Disdain would have made it easier to face the fact that hoping for a twist of fate was nothing but a whimsical notion.

But the pluses outweighed the minuses. Marcella had everything she'd ever dreamed of; a successful career, Brent's love, prospects for children and acceptance in her love's family.

Be strong, she ordered herself. She must do her best to give Brent at least a fifty-fifty chance.

Over the days that followed, Brent had never been happier. Or sadder. He and Cella were living with a truce, he mulled while sorting through paperwork in his cabin at the drilling site. She was sweet and mellow and loving. Yet by her tight-lipped attitude toward his wildcatting ventures, it was as clear as the sky outside the window that she wasn't one bit closer to accepting his occupation than she had been on the day of Jerry's accident. And he had a suspicion that it was the calm before the storm.

Brent tried unsuccessfully to concentrate on the work that lay on the table, his makeshift desk. Nothing was settled with Nevill Rogers.

On top of that headache, he had phoned the Houston bank about a decision on the Crooked Horn loan.

It appeared that the loan officer who had been handling his application got himself fired for some reason. Not that Brent was surprised. The guy had screwed up the paperwork for the ranch loan. Another officer, a female this time, was having to start from scratch in making a determination. She promised to have an answer for Brent in a week.

That was about seven days longer than RSK could afford.

"Say, Cap'n," Jerry said, cutting into Brent's brown study. "Have you had any word from Rogers on the new leasing agreement?"

"Nothing positive. Cella took care of the cashier's check Monday morning, and my attorney sent him the new contract by messenger that afternoon. I talked with the old geezer, but he's dragging his feet."

"That fifty thousand bucks sure did cut into RSK's operating funds," Jerry commented. "You had to pay Amigo Drilling and several big invoices. Payday's coming up, too."

"What are you getting at?"

"You need to give strong consideration to taking me in as a partner. My buddy in Houston has the cash. He's eager to advance me the money RSK needs."

"Unless Nevill agrees to our new terms, it makes no difference. We won't be drilling."

"Now, Cap'n, I have all the faith in the world you'll settle with Rogers."

Brent ducked his head and rested his forearms on the table. If the loan didn't come through, Jerry was the only answer.

He rubbed the back of his neck. "I'm expecting a deal to come through any day. If it materializes I won't need your money."

"What kind of deal?"

"That's personal." Brent pushed himself up from the chair and walked across the room. "Give me a week, Jerry. If I don't have the money I'm expecting by then, I'll accept your partnership."

"Unconditionally?"

Brent nodded agreement. They awkwardly shook on the pact; Jerry's right arm was still in a sling.

"Gotta be going," the geologist stated. "Need to look over some data at the office."

Jerry departed for Port Merritt. Brent had no desire to leave. Not yet, anyway. He didn't know how to handle Cella's terrors; he still had Nevill and the RRC to fight; he'd agreed, conditionally, to Jerry's partnership.

Ambling outside, he needed to commune with that now inanimate object, the Rollins One. The maintenance engineer's crew was hard at work taking out their equipment. Needing to keep his mind occupied with something other than his troubles, Brent offered to help them disassemble pumps and hoses.

As the hot, sultry afternoon wound down, Brent's muscles ached from lifting and yanking on heavy mud-pump paraphernalia. Finally the chore was finished; the equipment was loaded on a flatbed truck. With the back of his hand he wiped beads of grimy sweat from his brow as he straightened to a standing position.

Brent's line of sight swept upward. The Texas sun beat down on his face and unbuttoned chambray shirt. Amigo Drilling's operations had ceased. The diesel engines were silent; Brent missed their sounds and smells, among other things. No floor men pulled chain around drill pipe to "make a trip." The hands had moved on to another site. The Rollins One was desolate—*desolate*.

But hopefully this was a temporary setback.

God, he needed Marcella! A niggling suspicion crossed Brent's mind that their problems were permanent. Damn! Her attitude about his way of life was unreasonable.

"Say, Coulter," the maintenance engineer called, slicing into Brent's train of thought. "Thanks for pitching in."

"Nothing to it." He strode toward the rig floor.

Foot touching the first stair, he ground to a halt and turned to the sound of an approaching automobile. Brent ran his palm down the leg of his grease-covered Levi's, watching as Marcella stopped the car and got out. His pulse beating double-time, he stared. Over and over she had refused to visit the site again. Yet she was here of her own free will. Dare he hope that she had come over to his side?

He started toward her, but stopped. *She* had to make the first move. Her hair, wispy curls framing her beautiful oval face, was caught up in a bun at the crown of her head. Wearing a cream-colored linen suit, a dark blue blouse and with a corona of sunlight behind her, she looked like an angel.

Brent spoke not a word and neither did Marcella.

## Chapter Twelve

Twenty feet separated Marcella from Brent. To her those few footsteps might have been an ocean dividing her heart of hearts. On one shore she stood, defenseless against the inner turmoil of overwhelming love for him that demanded she face up to her professional and personal responsibilities to Brent. After speaking with Nevill Rogers about RSK, she had forced herself to drive out to the site.

Stalwart in his beliefs and dirty from oil, Brent waited on the other shore. Behind him was the strand of all he stood for as a wildcatter—the drilling rig and its promise for his company's future.

Wishing for a miracle that would transpose her into the woman he needed at his side, Marcella willed strength. She must bridge the gap parting them.

Slowly she opened her arms. He threw his hard hat to the ground and, with the warm vernal breeze ruffling his hair, sprinted to her widespread arms. As the full moon lures the seas, their spirits drew together and carried them above problems and insecurities as he crushed her to him. He was hers and she was his, and miracles do happen.

"Kiss me," he said, honey smooth.

Her fingers slid up the back of his damp chambray shirt, curling over his taut shoulders. The grease from his labors stained the ecru linen of her suit, but she didn't care. His eyes were filled with passion and questions. She inhaled the sharp odor of oil that clung to him and gave herself up to his loving embrace.

"I said kiss me, baby."

"My pleasure, darling." To a chorus of wolf whistles, her lips seized his.

"Your place or mine?" he murmured when she ended the embrace.

"Yours."

Then he was lifting her, swinging her. Waves of excitement beat through her veins as around and around she sailed, the pins flying from her hair.

"Put me down, Brent," she ordered, nonetheless exuberant in his presence. "We're making a scene."

"Who cares!" He swung her head down over his shoulder, steadying her with his powerful arms, and called to the workers. "I love her. Did you hear me? I love her!"

She pushed her tumbled hair from her face and giggled as her body jostled from Brent's footsteps as he carried her to his Bronco. "Hey, mister! Yes, you."

Pounding a forefinger against her beloved's back, she announced, "I love him!"

"You're a mess," he imparted later in the after-glow of loving.

In Brent's king-size bed Marcella leaned back on a pillow and held aloft his streaked forearm. "That's the pot calling the kettle black."

"Suppose we should've taken a shower before..."

"Brent Coulter, do you mean to tell me you would've taken time out for a shower?"

Chuckling, he curved a palm over her hip. "No. Are you offended?"

"For the first time in my life, a little dirt doesn't bother me a bit."

He was suddenly serious. "Cella, have you changed your mind about... about what I do for a living?"

"Let's take every day as it comes."

"You're stonewalling, Marcella."

"No, I'm taking your advice. You're the one who always talks about enjoying the present."

"My chickens have come home to roost," he said dryly.

It was clearly time to drop the subject. "Brent, I have good news for you."

"What's up?"

"I spoke with Nevill Rogers again today. He's agreed to your terms."

"All right!" Brent whistled in relief. "Money-grubbing old geezer. What in the devil made him change his mind? I talked with him this morning, and—"

"I used my feminine charms."

His gaze admiring, he caressed the lobe of her ear. "Heaven help the man who tries to fight your crafty wiles."

She was enchanted by his touch, and her response was whispered in her most provocative intonation. "Now, is that any way to talk about sweet little ol' me?"

"Don't you bat those thick lashes, woman. That's exactly what I meant." He plaited his fingers through her long black hair as he snuggled against her. "Why don't I give you a proper thank-you gift?"

"Later." She longed to succumb to their unquenchable physical thirsts. Simply being with Brent made her want to forget the outside world, but discussing the solution to Brent's problems with the royalty owner had brought other problems to mind. "What are you going to do for money?"

It was on the tip of Brent's tongue to spill the beans about the Crooked Horn loan. He knew he could trust her, but he bit off the admission. It wasn't a set deal yet; it might never be. "Take Jerry on as a partner," he admitted slowly. "At least it looks that way."

"Why, that's wonderful, sweetheart."

"That remains to be seen."

"It'll be all right. You'll see."

Wanting to comfort Brent, Marcella urged him to her. No matter how much she wished for him to get out of the wildcatting business, it hurt her to know that he was obliged to make concessions that he didn't want. Then, as comforting turned to passion, even these thoughts were driven from Marcella's mind.

\* \* \*

With the RRC's approval the petroleum exploration company was back in operation. Brent had moved quickly, cutting through red tape and rallying contractors, Marcella recalled five days later as she left Goodman National at the stroke of five to drive home.

Her house would seem empty; Brent wasn't expected until later that evening. As she turned onto the coastal road leading to her duplex sunlight reflected off the precious stones of her engagement ring. Warmth filled her each time she looked at the emerald-and-diamond antique. It was beautiful and fit so right on her finger! And to her it meant the world that he had given her the family heirloom and its promise.

Nevertheless, their wedding date still wasn't set. She refused to make definite plans until she could deal with the problems that plagued her. Would Lady Luck ever smile down and change Brent's line of work or, better yet, allay her terrors for his safety? No miracles to that point had been forthcoming.

Approaching her wood-framed home, she grabbed the garage door opener from the seat next to her and veered her car into the driveway only to see that already the overhead door was open. Her brows knitted as she stopped and got out of the sedan.

Brent stood in the shadowy garage with an array of gear around him including a piece of furniture that she recognized as the cradle she'd lost out on at the auction! What in heaven's name was going on?

She slammed the car door and ran toward him. "What are you doing?" she asked, a broad smile curving her lips.

"Going nuts." Grinning, he wiped his hands on a rag, then traced his now-clean finger along her chin. "Never let it be said I renege on a promise."

"Renege on a promise?"

"For helping me with Nevill, remember? I bought you a thank-you gift."

"I don't need thanks." Her words were truthful, though wrenching. "I'm happy everything went okay with Rogers and the Railroad Commission."

"I couldn't have made it without you."

"I did what had to be done." To get a better look at his purchase, she craned her neck to see around his tall frame. Atop a thick layer of gooey, dark-stained newspapers, the Victorian cradle sat. "Where did you find it?"

"Elementary, my dear Parker. I slipped a twenty to the auction house secretary for the dealer's name. I got in touch with him, set a price and then drove up to Austin this morning to buy it." He bowed low, his arm sweeping toward the crib. "And the rest is history."

"You big devil." Her palms slid up his chest, and she reached to kiss his smiling lips. "Thank you." Her heart was brimming with all she felt for Brent. Resting her cheek against the warmth of his shirt, she cuddled into his strength. "Brent darling, you are sweeter than a peach."

"Come on," he urged, pulling her arm. "Let's take a look at that thing."

Assessing the damages, Marcella crossed her arms. Old finish bubbled the rocker surfaces; long scrape marks exposed naked wood on the sides.

Cans of paint remover, paint and turpentine—all the wrong chemicals for refinishing a fine piece of walnut—were scattered around the crib. Amid the rubble was an electric sander as well as scrapers, screwdrivers and several sheets of—horrors!—heavy-weight sandpaper.

It was a refinisher's nightmare.

"Have to admit, though," Brent said, "I'm new at this business."

Chewing the inside of her cheek to keep from giggling. Marcella swallowed, unable to reply. She was not going to tell him that he was going about it the wrong way.

"This old finish is tough to get off." He grabbed a scraper, bent down and gave the wood a gouging swipe. Then he paused to study the results critically. "I could use some advice."

Leaning over, she pulled his head against her shoulder. Her body shook as happy laughter rang through the air. "Brent Coulter, I adore you."

"That's music to my ears, baby." Laughing, he fell to the cement floor, bringing her with him and cushioning the fall. "You're not going to believe this, but I've enjoyed fooling with that cradle. But I don't think I've been going about it the right way. Maybe you could show me, and we can work on it together."

"Deal."

"I hope we put that baby bed to good use someday," he whispered.

"So do I," she returned, her heart in every word. Marcella planted her elbows between his arms and ribs, regarding him happily. "Maybe you could take me fishing in the meantime."

"What! You're ready to 'murder' one of God's scaly creations?"

"I'll give it a try. But I'll draw the line at game hunting." She smiled tenderly. "The main thing is being with you."

"I second that." His palm rubbed up and down her back. "Let's make a point of concentrating on the things both of us enjoy: the sea, open air, home life. Especially home life."

"Since you put it that way, Brent, we're not really that different."

"And we're both driven to succeed at whatever we undertake," he added. "Not a bad combination, baby."

"Not a bad combination at all."

Her blue gaze locked with the green of his, and her fingers wound through his thick flaxen hair. His lips parted slightly as he brought his face upward. She met his embrace ardently. He groaned her name into the interior of her mouth as his lips and tongue stoked the wildfire within her.

"Why don't I get the door," he suggested hoarsely.

"You're full of wonderful ideas...."


Marcella's emotions were mixed the next afternoon. She was on cloud nine with love for Brent. But she was at her wit's end. Away from Brent's mesmerizing presence, each time she thought that she could deal with his profession, a hellish specter of Jerry's body flying through the air vividly filled her consciousness.

Nothing, barring a miracle, was going to change Brent Coulter's profession. But she had to hold on to the thin thread of hope that the hand of fate would alter his way of thinking. Or hers.

Sharon Bates popped her head through the office doorway. "Marcella, Jerry Hagen's here to see you."

The geologist was the last person Marcella wished to deal with at that moment, but she marshalled her businesslike aplomb. "Tell him to come in, please."

Standing, she greeted the man who was, like Brent Coulter, one of her customers. Once more seated behind her desk with Jerry across from her, they chatted amiably.

"Marcella, I need a loan," Jerry said, bracing his good arm on the desktop.

"We're always happy to accommodate our customers, Jerry. How much do you need and what do you need it for?"

"Three hundred thousand to buy into RSK."

"You're not serious!"

"Oh, but I am."

"What happened to your backer in Houston?"

"He changed his mind."

"Why?"

Jerry shrugged. "He invested elsewhere."

Considering Brent's adamant opposition to accepting help from his former father-in-law, Marcella shuddered to think what must be going through the wildcatter's mind. "I assume Brent knows you've come to me for a loan. What was his reaction?"

"He doesn't know about it."

"That's underhanded of you, Jerry. Even if it would be your responsibility to repay the debt, you know Brent has too much pride to accept Goodman National's help."

"He doesn't have to know about it. As soon as the Rollins One comes in, I'll repay the loan."

"And if it doesn't?"

"It will."

"And what do you plan to use for collateral?" she asked.

Jerry picked up a paper clip, appearing to study it. "My good name."

"Jerry Hagen, no lending institution will loan you that kind of money on your signature!"

"Goodman National will."

"Oh, no, we won't."

"Then you'd better talk to Sneed Goodman. I have. I went to him first. He'll okay the loan. But his hands are tied. Since you're the officer in charge of my personal account, it's up to you to put it before the Loan Committee."

That was the truth. As it stood presently, she couldn't turn her back on her responsibilities.

"Check with Sneed," Jerry continued.

"I'll have to get back with you."

"Thanks." Smiling, he stood. "I'll see my way out."

The door closed behind him.

Oh, Lord, she was in a predicament, her situation untenable. Brent would be livid with rage when he discovered, and he was sure to discover, that Jerry had applied to Goodman National for money. She cringed, thinking of how furious Brent would be to know that she had a hand in the deal.

But, she reasoned, RSK was limping along on the last of its ready cash. Surely Brent's fierce sense of pride wouldn't keep him from completing the Rollins One, no matter where the needed funds came from. Once he accepted the fact that Jerry's money was the only alternative, he would yield to the inevitable. He was too responsible to let his employees down. Moreover, he was too set on his dream for success to let anything stand in his way.

And as it stood it was her official duty to present Jerry's loan before the committee. But logic told her that it would be vetoed. Or would it? She needed to consult Sneed Goodman.

Seated across from the bank president in his office, she quickly cut to the heart of the matter. After relaying Jerry's request she sat back and waited for Goodman to respond.

His brown eyes never wavered as he said, "We'll give him the money."

"Why?"

"I love Brent Coulter as if he were my son," Goodman admitted. "If he would allow me, I'd help RSK. But he won't. He's too stubborn to let me do anything for him."

"I realize that."

"When he wanted to start out wildcatting, I advised against it," Goodman stated. "But he wasn't to be stopped, and I sponsored him. Covertly. For reasons I'd rather not discuss, I've been unable to provide the additional help he needs."

Such as, at his daughter's request, backing out on the original loan with the Corpus Christi bank, Marcella remembered from the anonymous letter Brent had received.

He leaned forward, resting a hand on his knee. "Ms. Parker, put Hagen's loan application before the committee."

"Sir, if I do I'll be betraying a trust our depositors have in me. If the well doesn't become a high-yield producer, Goodman National will suffer a great loss of money."

"We won't lose any money." Leaning back, he pressed his fingers together in a thoughtful gesture. "There's something else you should know. Geological tests were run on Nevill Rogers's property years ago. Rogers didn't want to drill on his ranch, but his wife had dollar signs in her eyes. She insisted. Just before drilling was to commence, Mr. and Mrs. Rogers divorced. He canceled the drilling plans, but in the divorce decree he had to make a huge settlement on her because of the geo tests."

"And if by some chance the tests are wrong...?"

"I'll make restitution out of my own pocket." He smiled widely. "But that day won't come."

"How can you be certain?"

"Rogers was banking with me back then. Brent stumbled on to the divorce papers, and he knew to go after the lease. Believe me, no one but Brent could've talked him into a drilling program. I have no doubt his exploratory well'll strike that underground lake of oil. But Brent needs cash. And Jerry Hagen is the solution. Don't you agree?"

"Yes, sir, I do," she responded quietly.

The conversation ended, Marcella left the president's office. She held the key to RSK's chance for success or assured failure. As vice president of the bank, she must perform her duties without consideration to her personal wants and needs.

Without the alliance RSK would go under. Although bankruptcy would force Brent to change occupations, he would be devastated to lose his hopes and dreams. And if Brent wasn't happy, she wouldn't be happy.

Resignation settled within her. Marcella's love for Brent superseded her own desires. He deserved the opportunity to fulfill his potential, and she would do everything in her power to insure it.

Brent should be advised about Jerry's plans, she surmised. In view of the direct effect the loan had on Brent, it was her duty to tell him.

And she also realized that no miracles were forthcoming—time had run out. It wouldn't be fair to tie him to her insecurities. For her own sanity she had to step out of Brent's life.

But first he had to be told of her decisions.

## Chapter Thirteen

As if in a daze, Marcella journeyed from the bank to Brent's duplex. The thought of breaking their engagement wrenched her heart, but she had no other choice. And Brent had to be apprised of the loan that would ensure RSK's future.

She entered the living room after his booming "Come in." Standing in the doorway, she painted an indelible picture of him in her mind, a memory to hold on to and cherish for the rest of her life. Broad of shoulders and lean hipped, he sat on the sofa with a mountain of drilling logs on his lap, his bronzed chest illuminated by the dim lamp glow and his chiseled cheeks and deeply cleft chin cast in muted relief.

Her golden god was smiling at her as he levered away from the sofa, papers scattering to the carpet when he stood to his formidable height and crossed the floor.

Beyond the physical, he was a good man, kind and generous. Loving and affectionate. Wildly passionate, yet tender. A perfect man.

Suddenly he stopped. "Why the glum expression?" he asked, his voice gravelly, as if he sensed the portent of her visit.

Ahead was the precipice of their future. Could she take that plunge from which there would be no turning back? She must. And she had to sacrifice her own chances for happiness by giving him the freedom to thrive as an independent oil man.

Touching the thick mustache that had always fascinated her, she shivered as she began to feel that familiar pull toward him. Her ambitious plans to step out of his life were weakening.

"Brent, I love you," she stated raggedly.

"Then whatever it is, it'll be all right. I'll make it all right."

"It's...it's not that easy, darling." She dropped her chin. "I—I've made some decisions."

"I don't like the sound of that." His palms cupped her face, compelling her to look at him. "You're not giving up on me, are you?"

She couldn't answer.

"Answer me."

"Jerry's friend backed out on financing his partnership."

He observed her suspiciously. "How come you know? Why didn't Jerry tell me himself?"

"He...he asked me for a loan to finance the deal."

"I trust you told him no."

"I'm in no position to do that."

"You know I don't want any part of Sneed Goodman's money! I won't grovel at his feet—it's a matter of pride with me."

"You aren't groveling at anyone's feet! It's Jerry's loan, not yours."

His fingers moved to clamp on to her shoulders. "Don't do it, Marcella."

She turned away from him. "I have to. You need money."

"When did you promise him a decision?"

"The Loan Committee meets tomorrow."

"Hold off on it—at least for a week."

"I can't."

"All I'm asking for is a few days."

"You're going to be flat broke in a week."

Brent opened his mouth as if to say something, but he didn't. Charging across the room and back again, he raked his fingers through his hair.

She moved in front of him. "Don't let your ego keep you from completing the well."

"Wait a minute! Jerry doesn't have sufficient collateral for a loan big enough to help RSK."

"I, uh, that's true."

"Does Sneed know about this?"

"Yes," she admitted raggedly.

"And they pressured you to handle the loan. The bastards!"

"That's not true. Brent, I have to ask you something. Knowing that Goodman National provided the funding, would you accept Jerry's partnership?"

He took a long time answering. "We have a gentleman's agreement. Look, I know how you feel about your job and I wouldn't ask this of you in a normal situation, but please stall him for a week." When she didn't reply he squeezed her elbows roughly. "Please don't let me down, Cella. I'm counting on you, do you understand?"

"Yes."

"Tell me something," he demanded. "Why are you even considering giving him money? Why did you help me with Rogers?"

"I have a professional duty to Jerry. I'm in charge of his account, and I don't conduct business on personal whims." Her voice lowered. "And I helped with Rogers because I love you."

"But don't you have everything to gain if RSK goes under? Then you'd have me on your own terms."

"You wouldn't be happy. And we'd both be miserable."

"Then promise me you won't do anything yet." He shook her lightly, then hugged her to him. "Promise me."

"I promise," she answered, knowing that any further arguments would be for naught. She couldn't fight his stubbornness; she would have to deal with the matter in the most sensible way. She would go through with the loan, though the thought tore her to shreds.

Then his face lowered to hers, his mouth touching her lips, first with a demand, then with tenderness. More than anything she yearned to have one last time in his arms before it was all over. "Make love to me, darling."

Brent embraced her as if he could never let her go. And she was falling, tumbling into the passion that could not be denied as his lips touched hers once more and his tongue probed the silkiness of her mouth. Her body melted against his and spoke a thousand words of desire. And he was lifting her, carrying her to his bed . . . for this one last time.

He undressed her slowly, reverently. Then his shadow fell over her as he unbuckled his belt. She watched, dazed, as he slid trousers and briefs down his muscular legs. Even though she craved the joining of their bodies and spirits, there was a grieving ache in her heart. This would be the last time they would love each other in life's most intimate way. Never again would she feel Brent's flesh against and inside hers. She would never experience the joy of having his child beneath her heart. And she would never grow old with Brent. A tear spilled from her eye. She had to relinquish the ties that bound them—for both of their sakes.

Brent leaned to brush the moisture from her cheek. "Don't cry. Please don't cry."

Her tears were now a cascade. "I can't go on—I can't go on."

"Oh, baby." He aligned his body with hers, comforting her.

"You can't give up your dreams for RSK," she admitted brokenly, "and I can't deal with my fears for your safety. There's no answer for us as a couple. Just hold me . . . please hold me."

Fearing she was right, Brent silently held her. There was no answer, unless he gave up all that he'd worked for. He wished with all his heart that he could make that move. And because of his inability to change, Cella was slipping away from him, not physically but emotionally. He was losing her. Losing her!

Someway, somehow he would find a way to keep her in his life and in his arms. He wouldn't give up hope—

couldn't give up hope!—and he was going to love her forever and ever.

Desperately he pulled her to him. She was warm and soft and velvety. Her hands were touching him in all the places that drove him beyond the realm of this world. He couldn't lose her! He buried his head into the fall of her midnight black hair, inhaling the sweet scent of her, ingraining her into his being. And he despised himself for not being able to give up success for love.

His eyes searched hers. Anguished yearning rocked him as he clung to her slender body. He wanted to have her at his side through eternity. He wanted to see her tummy swollen with his child, wanted to witness the miracle of that birth, wanted to shower his wife and family with all the love and protection he had to offer.

As if there were no tomorrow, he captured her lips in a kiss of love and pain and sadness. He could feel the rapid beat of her heart; his was hammering in rhythm. With a longing born of disheartenment, he wanted to plant his seed in her womb, wanted to know that his child was growing in the place where he'd found heaven on earth. Then he would never lose her. Never.

A strangled cry tore from his chest as he plunged into the cloak of her womanhood. She was meeting his demands, and he rejoiced in the sound of abandon that rippled from her throat. Her nails dug into his shoulders as they reached the height of primal wonder...and slowly descended to the sorrow of impending loss.

"I wish this moment never had to end," he whispered against her ear, damning the conception-preventing pills he'd forced her to take.

Then he felt shame as he nestled her body against him. Sweet mercies, he'd been ready to tie her to him with a child. Oh, she wanted children... and him.

But she couldn't cope with Brent Coulter, the wildcatter.

By morning Brent had come to a conclusion. He hadn't lost Cella! Maybe she couldn't admit it, even to herself, but she'd planned to go out on a limb *for their future.*

For an instant it came to mind that she might put Jerry's loan before the committee. No, she wouldn't do that. She had given her word of honor—under duress, of course—but she was a woman of integrity... one of the character traits that Brent liked best about her.

Striding through the entrance to Goodman National Bank, Brent was on top of the world. He had news—not just news, great news!—to share with Cella. And it wasn't only the super fact that his secretary, Crickett, had recovered from her injuries and was back manning the office.

He walked past a line of depositors with his head in the clouds, figuratively speaking. Dusting his sleeves, he stopped in front of Sharon Bates's desk.

"Top o' the morning. Cella in?"

The young secretary blushed, but grinned nevertheless. "She's in a meeting right now, Brent."

"I'll wait for her." He started to drop onto one of the benches that lined the wall. Bernice Prothro's voice stopped him, and he turned to her.

"Why, Brent Coulter, how are you?"

What was this? Bernie acting pleasant? Something was up. Just the same, Brent wasn't going to look for hidden meanings. "Uh . . . fine."

"Aren't you looking handsome today." A smile pulled up the woman's face as she patted his arm, motherly fashion. "Isn't he, Ms. Bates?"

"That he is," Sharon replied dryly, then she blushed.

"Waiting for Ms. Parker, Brent?"

"Uh, yes."

Another maternal pat to his arm. "Well, she's busy right now. How about a cup of coffee in my office?"

"Sure thing, Bernie." He gallantly offered her his arm.

Bernice Prothro's office resembled a war zone, he noted as she poured two cups of thick black coffee. The poor woman was probably working too hard, didn't have time to get herself organized. Funny. No matter how hard Cella worked, *she* was always the epitome of organization.

He scalded his tongue on the first sip. "Delicious," he praised, trying to swallow the pain.

"Why, thank you," she purred, dancing her fingers against her scrawny chest. "Anything to please."

He wasn't fooled by her phony airs. She definitely had something to say. And he bet a buck it wasn't to his advantage.

"Bernie, you've never had a kind word for me in our long history together." He drained the plastic container. "What's up?"

"Brent Coulter, don't you dare question my motives. You're a customer. It's my duty and privilege to see to your comforts while Ms. Parker's in the Loan Committee meeting.''

"Oh?''

"Oh, yes. The committee may be tied up for quite some time. They're deliberating over Mr. Hagen's loan.'' Bernice thumped the heel of a palm against her forehead. "Why I bet that's why you're here—to await the outcome!''

He crumbled the empty Styrofoam cup within his hand.

"My goodness, you're as white as a sheet.'' Bernice's razor-sharp words bit through him. "You did know that Ms. Parker was presenting Mr. Hagen's loan to the committee, didn't you?''

Brent stood, his eyes drilling holes through the malicious woman. He straightened his back and left her office. Hurt pierced the wall of his heart.

*Get control of yourself!* But he was powerless to control his rage. He had asked Marcella to wait on Jerry's loan for a few days. And she had gone ahead heedlessly.

The meeting was winding down. Marcella tried her best to ignore the pounding in her skull. No matter what she had resolved the evening before, she needed Brent in her life. Yet she was burning her bridges behind her. She had made a promise to him that she wouldn't be able to keep.

There was no other way to help RSK; the exploration company was perilously short of funds. Brent was playing for time that he didn't have. When she had asked him if he would accept Jerry's partnership even if the money came from Goodman National, he had told her of the "gentleman's agreement.'' Though he would no doubt be angry, Brent would keep his word. She had to put forth Jerry's application—if not for her professional obligation, for Brent personally.

Sneed Goodman headed the long, oval conference table. Marcella sat at his left, and Wayne Alvarez, the executive vice president, to his right. Craig Cook, vice president in charge of installment loans, poured a glass of water from the pitcher. Cigar stuck between his teeth, the cashier, Anthony Holt, leafed through a computer run.

"Are there any other prospective loans to be discussed?" Goodman asked, raising an expectant brow at Marcella.

How easy it would be to tell him no. Again Marcella searched her soul about presenting Jerry's loan before the members. She would be going against her promise to Brent.

"That's all for me, Sneed," Alvarez stated.

Craig Cook turned a palm up. "Ditto."

"Marcella?" Goodman said, looking at her strangely.

"One more, sir." Pushing her chair back, she stood. "Mr. Jerry Hagen has applied for an uncollateralized business loan in the amount of three hundred thousand dollars."

A round of low whistles and widened eyes settled on her. Unsecured loans of that magnitude weren't commonplace.

"Gentlemen!" Sneed Goodman pounded the table. "Control yourselves."

Marcella brushed an imagined strand of hair from her temple. "May I proceed?"

"By all means," Goodman conceded.

Minutes later the assemblage was solemn.

"Since Ms. Parker's placed this loan before the committee, she'll be the last to vote," the president stated unnecessarily. He picked up a pen to record the results. "As head of this financial institution, I vote yes," he said, his tone brooking no argument with his employees.

Wayne Alvarez squirmed. "Yes."

"Yes." Craig Cook was obviously less than pleased.

Anthony Holt's mouth lifted above his cigar as he eyed with disapproval the only female present. "Yes," he said on a puff of smoke.

They all turned to Marcella.

She looked with unseeing eyes past the other officers to the window. "Yes."

Marcella was last leaving the conference room. She needed a few quiet moments to collect her thoughts. Leaning against the high-back leather chair, she closed her eyes. It was done. Jerry had his loan, Brent would finalize the partnership agreement between the two of them and RSK could complete the Rollins One.

And Brent's faith in her would be destroyed. Though she had to separate herself from her love, it was crushing to come to grips with the reality that he wouldn't cherish memories of her. As she would of him.

Her shaking hands picked up a stack of folders; even shakier legs stepped to her office. Her eyelids dropped as she closed the door and wilted against the barrier. She had faced adversity and loss in the past, but nothing had left the emptiness now sinking through her.

The click of a cigarette lighter sounded from the corner. Without opening her eyes she knew the person in her office was Brent. Gathering her strength, she faced him. His suit-clad body was stretched out on the sofa.

"You did it, Marcella." Fury was written in every plane of his face as he brought the cigarette to a mouth compressed into a hard line.

Unable to grapple with his black look, she moved to her desk and dropped the folders. "Yes."

"Why?" Lightning fast he surged to her side. His fingers dug into her shoulders. "Marcella, dammit, why!"

"RSK needs money, and you didn't have a week to spare."

Ice dripped from his voice. "You should've let me be the judge of that."

Her sorrowful eyes met his glowering countenance. "I'm sorry." Then, ducking her head, she inched away from him and folded her arms to clutch her elbows.

Stepping in front of her and bending, he hissed his breath against her face. "For your information, Lady Banker, RSK doesn't need Sneed Goodman's money. I mortgaged my ranch."

"Ranch? You never mentioned owning any property." Her heart sank even lower. "Why didn't you tell me?"

"Guess I figured it was none of your damn business." His eyes were full of pain and anger.

"I understand why you're upset, and I don't blame you." Her voice then held an impassioned plea. "Please understand that I never meant to hurt you."

"Goodbye, Marcella."

Brent turned on the ball of his foot, and he was gone. Gone.

## Chapter Fourteen

As the days crept slowly by Marcella performed her banking duties by rote. She called up her near-empty storehouse of strength during one-on-one meetings with her customers. On the outside she was her usual businesslike self. On the inside she was devastated without Brent's presence in her life.

The evening hours were even harder to live through. No more sounds came from his side of the house. No more did Brent's hearty laughter fill the air around her. No more could she cuddle against Brent's wonderful body. With every breath in her body she missed him.

In a weak moment she telephoned Brent's office, hoping for a reconciliation or, at the very minimum, a chance to apologize. She learned "Mr. Coulter isn't in, and we don't know when to expect him, Ms. Parker.''

Marcella dashed for the telephone each time it rang, but Brent never returned her call. He was through with her. She had lost him. Lost him!

The small pleasures that had comforted Marcella in the past—her job, her home—brought little solace. Her life was empty, as deserted as the adjoining duplex.

She supposed Brent was living in the cabin at the site or maybe in Corpus Christi. Whatever the case, he hadn't returned home. Of course, he was busy. No doubt about that, either.

The news was all over town, probably all over Texas. At 4,942 feet, RSK Petroleum Corporation had struck a vast pool of oil with the Rollins One. Crude oil was flowing at a rate to rival Spindletop. Twenty new exploratory wells were being sunk in the Rollins Field.

Brent Coulter was on his way to being a very rich man. And Marcella was proud for him. From his success she took a large measure of inner satisfaction knowing that he had achieved his goals and was happy, at least in his professional life.

He had to be hurting on the inside; he had loved her—she knew he loved her. And she had let him down.

Marcella realized that by her fault alone, she only had memories of her beloved to cherish. And his ring, which would have to be returned.

While padding through her kitchen on a Thursday evening she heard the doorbell.

"Please let that be Brent," she pleaded aloud, wishing...hoping.

Grinning impishly, a Coulter stood in the entry— Debbie. Marcella swallowed her disappointment.

"Hi!" Debbie raised her arm; her hand held a covered plate. "I hope you like fat pills, 'cause Mom sent homemade fudge."

Marcella rallied cheerfulness. "How thoughtful! I think that's just what the doctor ordered." She stepped back. "Come in, and welcome."

Marcella retrieved colas and ice. Debbie tucked her legs beneath her on the floor, and Marcella joined her. Chattering nonstop about school, Debbie dug into the chocolates.

Then she stopped eating. "Don't you like fudge? Mom made it for you. She wanted you to know she's thinking of you."

Astonished, Marcella's eyes widened. "She's very dear. You Coulters are special people. But I...I'm not very hungry."

"You're upset about Brent," Debbie said in the understatement of the year.

Nervously Marcella rubbed the back of her elbow. "Yes."

"He's been a bear lately."

"With his wildcatting successes, he should be happy."

"He's not." Debbie placed her half-eaten candy on a napkin. With sad eyes she stared at Marcella. "I know I'm just a kid, but I'm grown up enough to know that Brent won't be happy until you two get back together. We'd all be a lot happier. Our parents and I want you in the family."

But Brent didn't. And even if he did Marcella couldn't let go of her haunting past, couldn't forget her father's dying visage or Jerry's helpless screams. Repeatedly Brent's face was superimposed on those images.

"Too much water's run under the bridge, Debbie."

"Hey, didn't I tell you a while back that he gets glad just like he gets mad? He'll get over being mad at you. He's forgiven Jerry, so why wouldn't he forgive you? After all he doesn't *love* Jerry."

"Sometimes love makes forgiveness impossible." Marcella lurched to her feet. She stroked Brent's ring. "I need to ask a favor of you."

"Sure. Whatcha need?"

Marcella slipped the precious heirloom off her finger. "Will you..." She choked. "Will you return this to Brent?"

"Shouldn't you do that yourself?"

Blinking back unshed tears, Marcella shook her head. "Do it for me...please."

"All right."

Not knowing how much longer she could keep her composure, Marcella said, "Debbie, I'm kind of tired. Maybe we should call it an evening."

"Well, sure." Debbie stood and grabbed her purse. "Marcella, I'm your friend. If you want to talk sometime, please call me."

"That means a lot." Marcella hugged her warmly. "I appreciate your caring. And tell your mom thank-you for the candy."

Once more alone, Marcella dropped onto the sofa and rubbed her temples with the heels of her palms. She felt drained, boneless, bare of spirit—as bare as her left ring finger.

She tried to tell herself that being apart from Brent was the best course of action. He had lost faith in her, and she rued the day Jerry Hagen had asked for that loan, which he had never used.

Remembering the morning of the Loan Committee meeting, Marcella shivered. Never would she forget Brent's countenance of fury and disillusionment. That had to be the longest day of her life.

Deep in recollection, Marcella closed her eyes. An hour after Brent had left, Jerry Hagen had dropped by her office to sign the final loan papers.

"RSK won't be needing your loan," Marcella explained to Jerry. "Brent's secured financing elsewhere."

Jerry had a suspicious expression. "Does he know I came to you for money?"

"Yes, I told him."

"Why'd you tell him, Marcella?" Jerry asked, peeved.

"I had to. But, Jerry, Brent told me beforehand that he intended to honor his bargain with you."

"The terms of our agreement wouldn't have gone into effect until tomorrow."

"Oh, Lord, that's why he wanted me to stall on a decision." Suddenly angry, she crossed her arms. "Then why didn't you wait until then to ask for a loan?"

"Marcella, he's talked to bankers till he's blue in the face trying to get working capital. I honestly believed RSK's time had run out." He was sheepish. "I'm sorry I involved you in this. If there'd been any other way..."

Returning to the present, Marcella shot up from the sofa. Brent had forgiven Jerry; Debbie had affirmed the bit of information passed on to Marcella. The geologist, according to her secretary Sharon, was still on RSK's payroll.

Marcella's eyes settled on the wall separating their duplexes. She missed Brent! It was getting harder and harder for her to stay in Port Merritt. Everywhere she went and everything she did reminded her of Brent. Since no feasible resolution was in the offing, what was the answer? Move away and find another job? No. She couldn't keep running from her problems.

Nor could she trust her fragile emotions to live the life of a wildcatter's wife, even if by some miracle Brent walked back into her life. But Marcella no longer believed in miracles; they were impractical.

That didn't stop the ache in her heart.

Marcella slept fitfully that night. In the morning she was awakened by the shrilling of the telephone. Anthony Holt, the bank's cashier had a terrible summer cold and had called to ask her to open Goodman National.

"Beautiful day, isn't it, Ms. Parker?" the guard, Simms, asked later as he relocked the glass doors after admitting Marcella and Bernice Prothro.

For all Marcella knew, a hurricane could have been raging outside. "Yes," she replied dully, "quite beautiful."

"What's the matter, Marcella?" Bernice's tone was snide. "Something wrong in your personal life?"

Marcella ignored the question as she led the others toward the strong room. She noted the hour: seven fifty-nine. One more minute and the timed device would allow her to open the walk-in safe. She placed her purse beside the heavy steel door and mentally counted the seconds. Anything to pass time. As eight struck she maneuvered the tumblers in the combination as Anthony had instructed her.

The door opened to display drawers and sacks of cash. Stepping into the close confines, she heard a noise behind her.

"Simms?" she questioned, uneasy that the guard hadn't followed her in the vault. "Bernice?"

"All right, you two. Get 'em up!"

The bank was being robbed!

"Get your hands off—" The rest of Bernice's sentence was muffled.

"Hit the floor, woman. You, too, old boy!"

*Oh, my God!*

Eyes on the open door and careful not to make a quick move, Marcella leaned against the wall and shouldered the silent alarm. She was standing quite still when almost immediately a small-statured man, his face covered with a red ski mask, lunged through the doorway and thrust a gun into her face. She held her arms upward.

Tapping the cold barrel against Marcella's forehead, he snarled, foul-breathed, "Don't give us any trouble, lady, and no one'll get hurt."

The first law of bank robbery survival was to do as told. "I won't give you any trouble."

"Get out there and lay down flat." Moving aside, he motioned with the barrel, and Marcella sidled warily past him.

Her eyes scanned the corridor. The robber's accomplice, heavyset and wearing a blue ski mask, jumped up from where he had finished trussing Simms, who was on the floor face down. The masked man shoved a knee into Bernice's back and wound cord around her wrists as she, also, lay prone.

"I said get down there," the red-masked assailant barked, as he pushed Marcella down roughly.

Marcella dropped, twisting her ankle, and a shaft of pain shot up her leg. The blue-masked bandit then grasped her arms. Hemp rope bit into her wrists and ankles as she was bound securely and left with her cheek grinding into the gritty floor.

Apparently satisfied they would have no more trouble from the bank employees, both crooks disappeared into the vault.

Marcella spat a particle of dust from her mouth. "Bernice, Simms," she uttered in the smallest of voices, "are you okay?" She cut her eyes to Bernice and saw that she had managed to sit up against a wall.

The guard merely nodded.

"Yes," the older woman answered, fright in her voice. "And you?"

"I'm okay."

"Enough of that yammering!" the runt demanded from inside the vault. Then to his partner: "Let's get outta here."

"Right. Let's go."

Gray money bags under each arm, both men charged out of the safe, the stout bandit in the lead.

"You won't get away with this!" Robbery survival tactics obviously forgotten, Bernice brought her knees up and in a flash, kicked out her bound feet, hitting the bigger thug on the calf. Bags dropped; money spilled. The man hollered. He scurried to retrieve the loot, almost tripping his accomplice and causing him to drop the sacks he carried. Forgetting the bags, the smaller robber dug into his waistband for his gun.

The blue-masked man spun on his heel from where he squatted gathering up spilled money and knocked the gun from the other man's hand. "No! We ain't got no time for killin'."

Terrified, Bernice keeled over and landed close to Marcella.

"Button up, fat ass." The other robber's mean little eyes glowed as red as his facial cover, and his voice was full of venom as he reached down for his revolver. "I'm runnin' this show, and I don't take orders from you." Nevertheless he stuffed the gun back into his waistband and knelt. "Now get this up." He fell to muttering about dummies who let dames trip them.

On the floor, Marcella hunched her shoulders. She heard and saw booty being stuffed into bags. The men hastily stood up, clutching bulging sacks but leaving scattered coins.

Two sets of feet pounded away, making for the rear entrance of the bank, but Marcella's sigh of relief was premature.

From down the hallway the deep voice of the larger robber yelled to the other, "They got us covered! What're we gonna do?"

His cohort snorted, then laughed viciously. "Don't be an idiot. We got insurance—those three back there. If the cops don't do as we say, we'll use 'em for cover. Or kill 'em—one by stinking one."

Why, oh why, had she set off the silent alarm? Marcella agonized.

*We're going to die!* Marcella shook with terror lest the men return and carry out the threat immediately. She held her breath and listened as they moved father away, intent, no doubt, on checking the whereabouts of the police. She would at least have a small respite from the terror, she felt.

*Oh, Brent, I need you!* Shivering, Marcella realized that Brent had been right. Life is fleeting, and the hand of fate can strike anytime, anyplace. How could she have ever been so blind? Why had she worried about rig safety? Being here in the bank at this hour was more perilous than being on an oil rig.

Marcella had lived in an ivory tower of her own ideals, her own irrational fears. *Please let me have the chance to make amends with Brent!*

The head bookkeeper cut into her tormented thoughts. "Marcella—"

"Be quiet," Marcella whispered. The bandits weren't within earshot and were caught up in their dilemma, but caution needed to prevail. "Don't make matters worse."

Bernice's eyes were clouded. The two women lay almost side by side. "But I have to tell you something, in case we don't get out of here alive," she stammered in a whisper. "I hated you. I wanted to hurt you."

"Shh, don't talk." Unsettled by Bernice's frank remarks, Marcella lifted her head toward Simms. He, apparently, hadn't heard Mrs. Prothro.

"I *must* tell you. It was wrong of me, but I wanted to get even. You didn't make a mistake your first day here—I purposely didn't tell you about the authorization codes. Later I found the key to Goodman's personal files and went through them at night. I knew you liked Brent, and there was my revenge. I sent him a letter, told him Goodman backed out on his bank note. I let Brent know about Mr. Hagen's loan, too."

"Oh, Bernice," Marcella muttered, remembering the troubles the woman had caused Brent. Further, she recalled Bernice's attitude toward her. "Why?"

"I was jealous of you." She grimaced. "You had everything I wanted: job, youth, beauty. It wasn't fair.

I've worked for twenty years in this bank and it got me nowhere.''

Marcella glanced to see if the robbers were returning, then regarded the woman who was to be pitied rather than scorned. She couldn't hate Bernice. She must be extremely bitter over the injustices life had dealt her, Marcella thought. It was a shame she'd had to lower herself to dirty tactics. "It's okay, Bernice. There's nothing to forgive.''

"Bless you.'' Bernice Prothro shuddered, then crawled even closer. "I recognize the fat one. If you get out alive, tell them Willie Jones was one of the men.''

"Who?''

"Willie Jones. He was a guard here until last February. Must be how he knew to get in without tripping the alarm.''

Suddenly the small one yelled to the lawmen outside through a crack in the back door. "We ain't giving up! We're coming out—and we're gonna use the hostages for cover!''

Brent was on his way back from San Antonio, by way of his parents' house. Debbie had left an explanation note along with Cella's engagement ring, which lay coldly in his breast pocket. Damn! He didn't want to think about it.

Trying to forget Marcella, he'd spent three days in the Alamo city. Those days had been called "vacation.'' It had been the worst holiday time he'd ever had. Cella had never left his thoughts.

The past two weeks had been living hell. Hitting a gusher wasn't as sweet as he had always thought it would be. Not without Marcella at his side. Disillusioned, angry and resentful, he'd paced floors and smoked cigarettes until his lungs were scorched.

Brent lit another cigarette with the truck lighter. Perhaps it was better that he and Cella no longer had a future together. No. That wasn't true. Even though Brent couldn't contend with her irrational fears for his safety, what they'd shared was spiritual...everlasting.

"Aw, hell," he muttered to himself. "What's love without trust?"

How could he have been so wrong about Cella? He had trusted her, and she betrayed him. Each time he tried to reason with himself that she'd only been doing her job by putting through Jerry's loan, he reminded himself of her broken promise. Okay, his request had been selfish, and he should have told her about the Crooked Horn loan, but she knew how he felt about taking Sneed Goodman's money.

But none of those thoughts stopped Brent from loving Cella.

Wheeling his Bronco into RSK's parking lot, Brent's muscles tensed. Sneed Goodman's big black car was in one of the spaces. Brent stomped into the office to find his black-haired, former father-in-law rising from a chair.

A strange expression in his dark eyes, Sneed moved toward him. "Son—"

"What're you doing here?" Brent asked curtly. "And where are Crickett and Debbie?"

"Since you were expected any minute, I told your secretary that I'd wait for you and for her to go on to lunch. And Debbie's with Marcella."

"*You* told my secretary—What the hell's going on? Why is Debbie with Marcella?"

"The, uh, the bank was robbed this morning."

"Is Cella all right!"

"Yes. She's a little shook up, and her ankle got sprained, but she's resting at home."

Suddenly the anger and resentment that had eaten at Brent subsided. And for once he could identify with her anxieties about safety.

"I'm going to her," he said, turning on his heel. "Come on, Sneed. I need to lock up."

A hand clasped his shoulder, stopping Brent.

"Hold on a minute, Brent. Give me a few minutes."

"Not now!"

"You have the rest of your life to make peace with Marcella. We need to make peace, too. Five minutes is all I ask."

"It's all spilled milk and the least of my problems right now." Not wanting to discuss anything that didn't pertain to Marcella, Brent turned. "What happened at the bank?"

Sneed explained the events. "... and when the two robbers tried to get away, the sheriff and his deputies lit into them." He chuckled. "Those karate lessons you gave them came in handy."

Brent hiked a brow.

"Son, I'm sorry for everything. I only wanted to help you, but you always had too much pride to let me do anything for you."

Feeling the need for total honesty, Brent spoke. "You backed out on my loan with the Corpus bank."

"And I'll always regret it." Sneed wiped a hand across his mouth. "Brent, I'm a father. You know how Vicky is—she's selfish. I didn't want to do it, but she was hurt when you two divorced, and she worked on me. Can you understand my predicament?"

"The ways of love are funny indeed...."

"Yes, indeed." Sneed exhaled loudly. "Son, I've always believed in you. And I knew about the geological reports on Rogers's land. But you didn't want my advice with RSK. When it looked as if you wouldn't complete the well and Hagen's backer retracted his offer, I went to Hagen and asked him to be the go-between. By the way, he didn't want to go against your wishes, I pressed him to do it."

"But why?"

"Because I respect you. And even though you're no longer married to my daughter, I wanted you to succeed." Sneed grinned. "Besides, I'm in the business to make money—GNB would've made money on Hagen's loan. As a businessman, you can appreciate that."

"I've been a stubborn fool," Brent admitted as he clasped Sneed's extended palm. "I'm willing to let bygones be bygones... and to restart our friendship."

"Excellent idea."

Brent locked up the office, and Sneed returned to Goodman National. Over and over in Brent's mind as he raced toward the beach duplex, he realized that he had been a fool where Marcella was concerned, too. Ten to one, he decided, she had been scared that if Hagen's loan didn't go through, RSK would fail. How could he have gotten angry over a selfless act?

Marcella was cold, yet the sun broiled down through the cloudless afternoon to the wooden deck. Sprained ankle propped on a pillow, she rested on a chaise longue and hugged an afghan around her shoulders. A flock of gulls landed on the railing, and Marcella threw some crackers their way. The lonesome sound of swells breaking against the beach provided background for her as she mentally rehearsed the words she would use to plead with Brent for his forgiveness—if she ever got the chance.

Later, after her speech was down pat, Marcella turned her thoughts to Debbie. Brent's sister had been such a dear. When she'd learned about the robbery and that Marcella was home alone, the teenager had called on her, offering assistance.

But Marcella had realized that Debbie was expected at RSK and she had told her, "I'll be fine. Go on to work."

But all alone it was oh so lonely to look out over the Gulf of Mexico.

"Cella...."

Twisting her sore body awkwardly, Marcella smiled. The salty breeze tousled Brent's hair as he walked steadily toward her. She ached to smooth those flaxen waves with her fingers. Oh, it was wonderful to have the opportunity to at least look at him! She longed to have him in her arms.... But was it too late?

"Brent, how are you?" she asked gently.

"I'm fine— No! I'm not fine. I'm terrible. But how are you? How's your ankle?"

She lifted her Ace-bandaged lower leg a hair. "It'll keep me off my feet for a few days."

"Let me get you an ice pack. Are you thirsty? Hungry?"

"No, please. Brent, I'd be doing a lot better if you'd come sit by me."

"My pleasure." His clear, direct sight was fastened on her searching blue eyes. "It kills me to think you were at the mercy of those thugs."

"It's all over now. Best forgotten."

He knelt beside her. "I've missed you."

"I've missed you, too," she returned, suddenly shy and unsure of herself. "I must look awful."

"You could use a little spiffing up." Leaning his head first one way, then the other, he sized her up. "But I see definite possibilities."

She gained strength to go on with her rehearsed words. "I'm proud of you. I heard about the Rollins Field. Congratulations."

"I got lucky. I wasn't so lucky in love."

"Brent, I'm sorry about the loan. I didn't want to go against your wishes. I simply wanted to help you, and I, well, I jumped to a conclusion about your 'gentlemen's agreement.'"

"I realize that. Oh, Cella, you had every right to know about my ranch loan. I wanted to confide in you, but I couldn't tell anyone. I couldn't take a chance that word would get back to my mother."

"We were both wrong."

"I've started turning wrongs to rights. I had a talk with Sneed a few minutes ago." He squeezed her hand. "No, don't look like I'm going to bite you. Everything's okay. I let my ego stand in the way of true friendship. I'm a lucky guy to have him in my corner."

"I'm in your corner, too."

He didn't answer. Looking away, he squinted toward the sun. She watched his throat work as he swallowed hard. Oh, Lord, had she lost him for good?

His expression was heavy with pleading as he turned his handsome face once more to her. "Then be a part of my life."

"I want to be." Her fingers touched his soft mustache, then moved to trace the grooves that had deepened around his mouth in the past days. "I was so wrong, Brent, so very wrong about the future. When I thought my life was in danger, it finally dawned on me how blind I'd been not to listen to you. You were right. It's the quality, not the quantity of life that matters. We have to make every moment count."

Astonishment played across his face, then joy broke through to soften his angular features.

"Thank God. I never thought I'd hear you say that."

"Well, I did. And I meant it."

"I understood today what you'd been going through—hell. I won't ask you to live with the dangers of the oil field. I'll give up RSK." He lifted her hand to his lips and kissed her palm tenderly. "Pushing a pencil sounds like heaven, if I know you'll be waiting in the evening for me."

Deeply touched by his offer, she nevertheless replied, "No. I don't want to change you. I fell in love with a freewheeling wildcatter, not the person I wanted you to be."

He lay his head on her lap, his arms tightening around her waist. "Oh, Cella baby, I love you so much."

"And I love you." She blinked away the tears that had gathered in her eyes and held his face between her hands. "I'll do anything to prove it—live in the shadow of your rigs, give up my career—whatever it takes."

"I don't want to change you, either, Cella. Stay just as you are." Digging into his pocket, he looked deeply into her eyes. "Take back my ring and let's make a brood of little Coulters."

"I thought you'd never ask . . . again."

"I'll take that for an affirmative answer," he said, smiling as he slipped the emerald-and-diamond antique onto her finger for the second and final time.

"You bet." Her voice was wickedly seductive. "Come here, future husband of mine."

"I'll hurt you."

"No, Brent, the hurting is over."

And it was.

# COMING NEXT MONTH

**DOUBLE JEOPARDY—Brooke Hastings**
Ellie came to Raven's Island to take part in a romantic mystery-adventure game but soon found herself caught in the middle of a real romance and a real adventure where murder wasn't just a game.

**SHADOWS IN THE NIGHT—Linda Turner**
When Samantha was kidnapped, she knew there was little hope for her unless the handsome dark-haired smuggler risked his place in the gang and his life to help her escape.

**WILDCATTER'S PROMISE—Margaret Ripy**
Financially, Cade was a gambler, but emotionally he was afraid to risk anything. Kate had to convince him to take that one extra step and fill the void in their lives.

**JUST A KISS AWAY—Natalie Bishop**
At first it was a case of mistaken identities, but Gavin soon realized that Callie was the woman he should have been searching for all along.

**OUT OF A DREAM—Diana Stuart**
Tara and Brian were both trying to escape, and their chance encounter on Cape Cod was perfect, the stuff out of fantasies. But could the romance last when real life intruded? They had to find out.

**WHIMS OF FATE—Ruth Langan**
Kirsten couldn't forget the mysterious stranger who had stolen a kiss....
He was prince of the country and heir to the throne, and Cinderella is only a fairy tale. Isn't it?

## AVAILABLE NOW:

**A WALK IN PARADISE**
Ada Steward

**EVERY MOMENT COUNTS**
Martha Hix

**A WILL AND A WAY**
Nora Roberts

**A SPECIAL MAN**
Billie Green

**ROSES AND REGRETS**
Bay Matthews

**LEGACY OF THE WOLF**
Sonja Massie